THE SPACEJACKER TRIAL

AND OTHER SCIENCE-FICTION STORIES

by Richard Buchko

ISBN: 1440403732
EAN-13: 9781440403736

August 2008

Richard Buchko
109 Fifth Street #1
Calumet MI 49913
734-934-7036
richardbuchko@gmail.com

Photos throughout this book
Are NASA press photos discovered at a flea market in
Florida, not far from Cape Canaveral.

INTRODUCTION

The short story and science-fiction have always been suited to one another. In a short story there isn't always room for in-depth character development, intricate descriptions of a scene and a complete way-of-life, or an endless series of plot twists. If some of these can be included, so much the better, but these are literary points more often left for a novel. What a short story offers more than anything else is an idea. If, after reading a short story, you've been given something to ponder, that short story worked. If you've been shown a point of view you perhaps never considered before, or were able to experience an emotion from reading, or left wanting a little more, the story was even more successful.

Science-fiction, it's almost needless to say, is a genre of ideas. All the characterization in the world, all the description and detail of a civilization or universe in which a science-fiction story could take place, these mean nothing unless there's an idea around which to build the story.

For decades the short story was the mainstay of science-fiction. Writers made their living through stories in science-fiction magazines. Some used it as a stepping stone to novels, then later to movies and TV writing, but they were trained, their skills were honed and their names became known, through the short story. Ah, the variety and sheer number of SF short stories that were released onto the world in the 30's, the 40's, the 50's and well into the 60's! It would literally be impossible (outside the realm of science-fiction, anyway) for someone to read all the worthwhile stories created in those days.

But, sadly, those days are gone. Very few science-fiction magazines survive, and the short story is not longer that training ground or stepping stone to bigger things. Short story anthologies are poor sellers in today's bookstores, so fewer and fewer are published each year. Today the epic novel and the 7-

part series are popular; it's almost obligatory that any book be part of at least a trilogy.

The quality of science-fiction novels has suffered, and the reason is plain --- because the popularity of novels and epic has taken over science-fiction, very few authors understand the skill of conciseness. They have 100,000 words (or a million) in which to tell their stories, so they don't learn economy of language. Fatter books are not always better books.

There are many fantastic novels in modern science-fiction. The difference it perhaps just statistical – there are a higher percentage of poorer novels being published today, simply because there are a lower percentage of skilled writers creating them. Without the short-story as a vehicle, as a way for publisher to gauge an author's popularity and for the reader to develop a taste for a particular author's style, the genre has suffered.

Will the short story make a comeback in science-fiction? Probably not. Like many things – big cars, 8-track tapes, and radio serials – its day may have passed. Nonetheless, the short story and science-fiction remain suited to one another, and I hope that after reading this small collection, you'll agree.

KENNEDY SPACE CENTER, FLA. -- GEMINI #8 SPACECRAFT BEING HOISTED ONTO THE BORESIGHT TOWER. JANUARY 26, 1966

THE SPACEJACKER TRIAL

THE SPACEJACKER TRIAL -- that's what it came to be known throughout the galactic Tribes. Each news program and most conversation, on Renna and on all the planets of The Tribes seemed to be filled with the latest fact or rumor about this case and its unusual criminal. While the outcome seemed a foregone conclusion, people still grew anxious as the day of the trial approached. As Kron walked toward the judgment halls, he felt the stares of those he passed.

Kron wasn't happy about being assigned as defender. *You should be honored. It is a great sign of respect to be chosen in such a high profile case.* He had heard this often recently, but it was a lie; he knew exactly why he was chosen to defend this man of Earth. First of all, the case couldn't be won, so no one else wanted it. The criminal's own statements proved he was guilty. Earth did not belong to The Tribes, and her people were considered by most Tribesmen to be sub-intelligent. The nature of the crime, and the criminal's status as an offworlder meant that public opinion would be against him; and law, despite theories and claims of neutrality, was often a political machine. This case had worked its way down the ladder of power, finally resting with Kron, someone without the influence or the tenure to refuse it. Finally, there was Kron's stand on *Dangerous Motivation* crimes; he disagreed with the sentences, special punishments reserved for crimes committed for particularly threatening reasons. Since this was a severe *Dangerous Motivation* crime, by using Kron as defender there could be no later criticism that the Earthman did not have fair representation.

No, Kron had the case, he would lose it, and the results would be terrible.

The Tihn Judgment Hall stood as the largest structure on Renna, headquarters of The Tribes. Here was where Kron had spent all 15 years of his studies, learning the complex laws needed to govern a hundred species on a thousand worlds.

Four Rennite miles high, and nearly as wide, the Hall was impressive even after all this time.

Kron climbed the outer walls, veering away from anyone who might know him, until he reached the holding area. Outside the door stood a lone guard - not an impressive fellow, short, well past his prime years, and with an arm missing. Still, the other five arms looked strong enough to do the job if this criminal presented any trouble.

Kron opened the door, and saw quickly that there was not much chance of trouble. The defendant was a human - male, he supposed. The man sat uncomfortably in a chair much too large for him. He had only four arms, two of them dangled beneath him and seemed primarily for walking, as was true of most human types. Kron ambled over to the high table between them, raised his two upper arms, unfolded the talons in greeting and said, "Hello. My name is Kron. I will be defending you in this case."

The human said nervously, "I am Andrew Richards." He raised his upper arms also. Good, thought Kron. If he is to have a chance at all, it is best that he tries to learn the proper manner of behavior.

"What has been explained to you?" Kron asked.

The human stood and walked slowly about the small room. Kron recalled pictures of humanoids while he was in school, but had never seen one in person. A few human planets had been accepted into The Tribes, but Kron always heard that humans were among the most backward of peoples, and he marveled that they could move about on only two of their arms. "When I was rescued from the ship that took me from Earth," the human said, "the spider-people just brought me to this place. I was stuck in another room until a few minutes ago."

"Spider-people?" Kron asked.

"People like you, with all those extra arms and ---------legs."

Kron's translator typically worked instantaneously, but hesitated at the human's last word. Unable to find the proper

Rennite word or phrase, it offered only the human's word "leg." Kron ignored it, for now. "Have you been fed?"

"Yes - and told that I'm under arrest. Look - I didn't plan to fly off in that ship. I was just lookin' at it an' it blasted off. Hey, it was on my planet, you know! I think I have the right to look it over, but I wasn't tryin' to go anywhere in the thing!"

Kron shook his heads and closed his eye. When the human talked like that, admitting his guilt in the most obvious manner, it would be that much harder to save him. "Before you continue, Abdru Richarz, I will explain things to you more completely. You were-----arrested-----because you entered the spaceship of another being and through whatever actions you took that ship left the area where –" he searched for the name of the pilot in his papers, "- Prel-Ong-Thouf was investigating." Andrew started to speak, but Kron quickly lifted four arms to silence him and continued. "You violated one of the most severe laws we have: theft of a spaceship from an alien world. To those investigating offworlds like your Earth, the ship represents survival. We don't allow contact with beings from non-member worlds, so being stranded without a ship can mean death. Because of the inherent dangers in otherworldly investigations, your actions are tantamount to attempted murder. Furthermore, you freely admitted that you committed the crime, many times before I arrived, and once more a minute ago. Is this not true?"

"Yes!" Andrew belted, waving one arm about in a strange manner. "I never said I didn't leave in the ship, but I didn't mean for it to take off! I was scared out of my mind when it did, and I was even more scared when suddenly a bunch of ----- you people ---- came in and grabbed me. You see, it was an accident. I was just ------------"

The translator was unable to work on the final word. "Abdru, your case is very serious. I realize that you don't understand all of our laws, but you are still bound by them. You will stand trial, and I will do my best to defend you, but your chances are very poor. You committed a grave crime.

7

Also, your crime falls under *Dangerous Motivation* statutes."

Andrew stopped walking. "Dangerous Motivation? What's that?"

"It's the reason you took the ship. You were not out for profit in stealing it, which, though illegal, is considered by some member worlds to be less serious. You were not out for revenge or acting from fear or hate. These can be understood, but you can't use these as a defense. Your reason for committing the crime is much more serious; most of The Tribesmen cannot even understand it. I think I do, but that will not help. Finally, since your world is not a member of The Tribes, and considered a substandard candidate for membership, many of the Assembly will be looking for the most severe punishment available."

The meeting continued for another hour. The human eventually understood that he would not be looked upon kindly by the court that would try him. Kron discovered that the humans of Earth were not aware of The Tribes, or of any beings off their planet. Under normal circumstances that might help him, but Kron doubted so in this case. The human's actions were deliberate. Kron tried to guide him toward the proper words, nearly in violation of his oath as a defender, but the human again seemed not to understand, stood firm in his story. Indeed, he seemed to think his own version - the truth, he called it - would be his salvation. Amazing, Kron thought.

He ended the meeting. "Abdru-Richarz, I will do my best for you tomorrow. The trial will not take place today because we are experiencing difficulty in translating some of your words. It is critical that we have no misunderstandings during the trial, or the results could be disastrous."

Kron walked home slowly. *Years of study, and this is my fate!* Kron believed that he understood the laws of The Tribes as well as anyone, especially when it came to offworlders, but nothing he could devise would give the human a fighting chance. No strategy would work. He climbed the outer wall to his apartment, moved slowly through the tunnels and smiled to see his mate waiting for him inside.

"Hello," said Step-Pon-Baf. She intertwined her arms with his in consolation. "You don't look happy."

"I'm unable to win this case, Step-Pon-Baf. And I feel the *Dangerous Motivation* designation is unfair in this case."

"You always say that."

"But this creature barely understands the concepts of law; he has only one brain, and a small one at that. Should we expect lower animals to obey rules meant for intelligent beings?"

She tightened her grip. "He's human. I hear they are ugly, and fierce."

"Ugly, yes, but hardly fierce," Kron replied. "He stands only to mid-breast level, and not very muscular. He was covered by a strange film of fabrics, and no feathers. From what I saw, my dear, you could probably swallow him whole."

***

The trial was delayed an extra day to improve the translators toward human speech, so Kron met with the defendant again. He came away feeling more depressed. Finally, the time for the event arrived. The defendant sat alone in a corner, traditional seat for the criminal. They should have found a more comfortable chair for him, thought Kron, who sat to his right. To the left sat the judge, the trial secretary, and the complainant. In front gathered the Assembly. Kron could not remember the auditorium ever being so full as today. The crowd numbered in the thousands. Most were Rennites, but a representation from many worlds also came. In the first hundred rows or so, of course, holographic cameras took in every angle to provide coverage for all the concerned Tribesmen. Kron couldn't see the last rows. Somewhere in the crowd sat Step-Pon-Baf. He felt glad to have her. She understood his passions for the job, and tolerated his beliefs even when she, like most Rennites, thought them crazy. Most of the people in front of him wanted blood, and they would get it. Kron didn't like the human. Abdru certainly lacked a basic

9

moral understanding, and lacked the sense to lie about it. Still, Kron felt humans would amount to nothing more than an annoyance, if even that. To hold them up to the laws of civilized people seemed silly.

The human trembled.

The judge spoke to the crowd. "I have been instructed that our translators are attuned as closely as possible to the speech of the criminal. If there is a delay in translation, wait in silence and allow it to process the words. The complainant, Prel-Ong-Thouf attends, and the defender is Kron-Brods-Erg. Because the crime has been freely admitted to officers and to the defender, no prosecutor is needed. Kron, will you speak before your client is offered the opportunity?"

Kron stood, and walked away from his table. His left brain ached from the stress of the past two days. He stood close to Richarz, attempting to illustrate the tremendous difference in size between Rennites and humans, and perhaps to gain some sympathy. "The crime of *Theft of a Spaceship on an Alien World* is freely admitted," Kron began. "The criminal asks for what he calls 'mercy'. The translators have been unable to give us a meaning, but I interpret it as, 'like me even though I am unlikable'. My client does not understand our laws, and does not feel bound by them. While I obviously do not support that belief, I do feel that only the theft charge should be allowed. The *Dangerous Motivation* charge is unjustified. Humans, while one of the dominant species on Earth, are not capable of higher reasoning. Many of our domesticated animals would match or surpass this human in intelligence. They are millennia from being able to distinguish true right from wrong. I ask that the *Dangerous Motivation* charges be dropped."

Murmurs came from the crowd. The judge frowned and shook his heads. "Are you saying that the human did not know he was inside the spaceship which belonged to someone else?'

"No, sir. I am saying that he did not know that to enter it was a crime."

10

Some people laughed. Kron believed it was true that Abdru-Richarz saw nothing wrong with his actions - unfortunately that would more likely hurt him, because so many here wanted a conviction. It was mostly prejudice among the crowd, a way to inflate their own importance by conquering others. He doubted he could find one supporter among the crowd, including his mate.

"Andru-Rikarz," the judge said, "When you saw this man's ship, did you know what it was?"

Andrew's expression had not changed since the beginning of the trial, even when Kron called him unintelligent. He appeared shocked to have finally been directly addressed by the court. "I - I figured it had to be a spaceship of some kind. I'd never seen one before, maybe nobody had, but I knew it wasn't from Earth."

"Why did you think it was there -- as a gift to you?"

Water oozed from the human's skin. "No, I didn't think that. But I didn't know if anyone was there with the ship. It seemed deserted. I'd read stories, you know - stories where a ship arrives from nowhere and takes people away. Close Encounters, UFOs, you know - that kind of stuff."

The defendant wasn't making sense. The Assembly and the judge were becoming impatient. Criminals were seldom allowed to speak long, and the human's time was about up.

The judge trained his eye on the man. Realizing the spotlight he stood in, the judge rose and spoke slowly, deliberately. He realized that legal history was his to make, and like all good politicians he would seize the opportunity.

"The job of exploring offworlds is dangerous and noble. The possibility of being stranded on an alien world limits this task to only the bravest of men. You, Abdru-Rikarz, committed the most serious crime imaginable under these circumstances. You admit that you entered the ship. You caused it to leave the planet, and while you are not intelligent enough to operate the craft, your actions caused the leaving nonetheless. We are not here to decide if you did this, but to evaluate why. You could not profit from the ship - you did not know how. You do not know the complainant, so revenge is not a factor. What extenuating circumstance can you offer?"

The human paused to understand the translation, and then he spoke. "I was just ------"

Kron had heard the word before and hadn't understood it, but this time it took only a few seconds for the translator to process it.

"------------curious."

The crowd erupted. Many of the males screamed in anger. The females tried to control them. The judge sat, and the trial secretary did not even write the translation into the record.

Kron moved over to his seat, and lowered himself in utter defeat, all arms hanging limply across the table. It would have been better if the trial had been conducted before the translators were tuned.

The judge, again, spoke slowly and deliberately.

"I would ordinarily get an official opinion of the Assembly before rendering my decision, but in this case it is unnecessary. Human Abdru-Richarz, you are guilty of *Theft of a Spaceship on an Alien World*, and of a *Dangerous Motivation* crime. That you so freely admit ------ curiosity ------ and find no shame in it relieves me of the heavy responsibility I often feel while presiding over this court. Surely your people cannot be so unintelligent that you do not see the evil in your makeup.

"Curiosity as a driving force in criminal motivation disappeared from The Tribes over 300 years ago. This purposeless and reckless pattern leads only to death and pain. Crime and its destructive power can only be eliminated when the dangerous motivations are drawn out and destroyed. If you punish the individual criminal, however, the danger remains within the species. It is the decision of this court that you be returned to your planet. There, in order to end the danger you pose, and at a time to be scheduled later, elimination of Earth will begin. No measure is too severe to stem the evil tide of curiosity."

The Assembly cheered.

Kron felt very low.   He had tried to do his job. Hopefully no one would fault him for that, since the outcome was inevitable.   Step-Pon-Baf reached him through the crowd. "Are you okay?"

"Yes," Kron said, "but I will never understand this. Why would you destroy an entire planet because some of its people are—" He stumbled over the odd word, "curious?"

"Because, my love, we'll never be able to rid them of it. We cannot teach it out of them, and we cannot breed it out. I'm just glad we learned of it now, before they advanced technologically and could harm us."

Kron thought for a while.   He had to admit she could be right.   Better to eliminate them now.

Wasn't every being just a little that way, though ------ curious?

He kept that thought to himself.

END

JULY 28, 1964 - RANGER 7 LIFTED OFF PAD 12 AT 11:50 AM EST ON ITS 222,522 MILE TRIP THRU SPACE TO THE MOON. IF ALL GOES WELL IMPACT ON THE MOON WILL TAKE PLACE APPROXIMATELY 9:26AM EDT FRIDAY THE 31ST DAY OF JULY

DURING THE FINAL MINUTES OF FLIGHT BEFORE THE SPACECRAFT IMPACTS ON THE MOON TV CAMERAS WILL TRANSMIT SIGNALS BACK TO EARTH TRACKING STATIONS TO BE RECORDED ON MAGNETIC TAPE AND 35MM FILM.

THE MILLENNIUM PROJECT

The launch actually took place in the year 2043, but it had always been called THE MILLENNIUM PROJECT because the idea was secretly conceived in the year 2001. So much new hope was shared that year. Many decided, on reflection, that it was part of the collective sigh of relief from society, happy simply to have made it through the 20th Century. Others adhered to the faith in a metaphysical or spiritual magic of a new millennium. Others still just wanted a chance, however slim, of escaping the planet.

Frank Sorrell was born the day THE MILLENNIUM PROJECT was born. He never claimed that it made him destined for the project, but admitted that the shared birthdates was what made him first interested in it. It was his hard work that made him the Captain - that, and seven years of intense military and scientific training, the kind that resulted in countless washouts, and more than a few suicides. It was tough, but from the moment he heard about it Frank Sorrell wanted to be on the ship; now he would be, as Captain of the first interplanetary manned vessel, The Terran. The crew was small, and well trained, but he hardly knew any of them. They all manned a simulation together, but they were kept isolated from one another during most of their preparation. Ahead they faced three months together, in a ship which provided little space and less privacy, so the idea was to let them get to know one another during the flight - less chance of them getting tired of and hating one another.

In theory. What he saw of the crew made Frank Sorrel doubt the success of the pre-flight separation. Just this morning he learned that one member, the pilot James Biddle, would not make the trip. He had developed a minor infection, and the threat it posed to the ship was small, but no chances would be taken. The alternate, Gerald Hannah, had been assigned. Frank had never met him, but if he was anything like the rest it would be a challenging flight.

Sorrel sat in the back of the shuttle car, fidgeting and trying to pass the time by thinking about his duties. The small black vehicle bounced lightly on the surface of the moon, kicking up rocks and dust as the driver made his way toward the Reagan Space Center, across the flats of the Sea Of Tranquility, with the Earth lazily following them. They were still a half moon away from The Terran, at a secret location known to only a handful of scientists and technicians. To prevent sabotage, The Terran, the greatest experiment in interstellar travel, lay hiding in a crater. *Cowering*, Sorrel thought. *Some great experiment!*

The Reagan Space Center, headquarters of the International Space Alliance – ISA - appeared slowly on the horizon. To its inhabitants, off the record, it was known as *the decoy.* Sorrel could see teams working to repair the damage from the most recent bombing. ISA had evacuated the site after the explosion, which delayed the launch by another two days. It had been a small bomb, launched from somewhere in Europe, and was able to penetrate the defenses simply because it was so small. Still, it destroyed two labs, killing three. Had it been any more on target, the false launch site of a phony Terran spaceship, the crew would all be dead, because the missile had landed during their flight simulations.

Sorrel hated the politics, but he understood how it worked, and if he needed a reason to be glad he was taking this flight, other than his yearning to explore the galaxy, getting away from mindless death would be it.

The car slid into the tunnel entrance, and was slowed by controlled friction against the steel walls. The sound echoed through Sorrel's bones, as it always did. He hated it. As he said that to himself he realized that lately he hated a lot. He couldn't wait to be off the moon and deep into space.

Sorrel felt the car stop in the dark tunnel. The door slid open, and Mick Keller's hand reached in after him.

"We're in a hurry, Frank," he said as he pulled the much taller and much stronger Sorrel out of the car and into the building. Sorrel shook free as he gained his balance, but kept pace with the swift legs of the other man. Mick Keller's job was specialized - he was charged with knowing where every crewmember and all the alternates were, and with getting them where they were supposed to be at the moment they were supposed to be there. In many circles this would be a job for the lowest ranking officers, but Keller was a full colonel. Keeping track of over a dozen individuals, none of whom were allowed to be in the same place as another at any time without authorization, on a moon where every base, every settlement was a potential target, made it a job that required authority, strength of character, and intelligence. Keller had all three. Frank Sorrel yelled above the noise of shuttle cars moving cargo along their tracks. "What's going on?"

"The launch has been moved up."

"How soon?"

"As soon as you get there."

Sorrel stopped. The launch of Terran wasn't planned for another 24 hours! Mick continued running, even after turning his head to see Sorrel, so Frank understood that there was no point in waiting to talk. He noticed that the Reagan Center tracks were full of cargo trailers, small trains that moved all the material on the station. The corridors themselves were sparsely populated, but everyone was moving with an urgency he hadn't seen before. He resumed running.

"Why?" he panted as he finally caught Mick around a corner.

"Fear of more bombings. They think that the launch site may have been leaked."

"But it's on the dark side. What are the chances of blind-site bombing being successful?"

They ran full speed past a security checkpoint with no soldier manning it. Nothing was operating as it had for the past six months. The cargo tracks which ran along either side of the corridors were moving slowly, but they were all full. There wasn't this much activity, Sorrel thought, when the base was evacuated after the bombing.

Mick answered, "Don't know. All I can tell you right

16

now is that once you get to The Terran, it's out of here."

No more point in talking now, Sorrel decided. They would be spending an hour or two riding across the lunar surface. He wondered if the others were already there, since Mick was taking him personally. If so, why was he the last?

***

Armstrong Base - scheduled for construction during 2045.

In reality, the launch site. While the combined governments argued about the cost of another moon base, and the press wrote story after story about what it could mean, what it would do, Armstrong Base was made fully operational years before it was supposed to be started - one of the advantages of operating on the dark side of the moon. Less than a hundred people knew of its existence, all sworn to secrecy - with severe military punishments for breaking it - until after the launching of the interstellar ship Terran. The complex was a series of rectangular cells resting on gigantic steel and concrete pedestals driven deep into the lunar rock. The cells formed a horseshoe a quarter mile across. Inside the shoe, covered by a steel dome cleverly colored the same as the surrounding rock, lay The Terran. Whereas in the past nearly all the energies of a space mission were given to problems of safety and survival during the voyage, the modern politics dictated that at least as much energy - and money - be allocated toward security before the launch.

The ride to the base had been easy, but strangely quiet. Mick Keller offered no new information, and made himself busy enough to keep Frank Sorrell from asking too many questions. After a time Frank decided to sit it out. Nothing he could know or say would make a difference in the plans, and he would find out soon enough. The car rolled up to C Building, and an ensign in full space suit walked out from behind a steel door and manually secured the car to the outer airlock. After a moment the car door opened and the two men

17

walked into Armstrong Base. They passed quickly, Keller leading, through the docking area and moved into the main section of C Building. It resembled a warehouse, one big room filled to the ceiling with products. This cell was the first stop for all materials entering the base, passengers or cargo. Other sections contained the living quarters for those permanently stationed there, the science labs, and machining shops where parts which had no earthly purpose were manufactured. Frank had seen them all, but he apparently wouldn't stop in them today. Mick led him straight to the tunnel entrance - the only path which led to the ship.

"How soon is this launch?" Frank asked.

"Twenty minutes."

Frank grabbed the other by his arm and pulled him back. "Wait a minute, Mick. I haven't said good-bye to anyone. I haven't even packed."

"Everything from your lunar quarters is already on board. Look, Frank, I'm sorry about all this. I wish I could have told you more, sooner, but I only found out just before I caught up to you. There is a danger that the location of the ship has been leaked. Vienna is afraid of a possible strike. It's a slim possibility, but if anything happens this project wouldn't see another chance for ten years, if we could even get the funds to try. Terran has to launch, and to be completely safe she has to launch now."

Mick turned and continued down the dimly lit tunnel. Frank paused only briefly then followed. No matter, he thought, being honest with himself. He had no one to really say good-bye to, and preferred it that way. A lot was unknown about this mission, and even the best estimates said that no one alive on Earth right now would be here when the ship returned, if it returned at all. Over the past several years alternative theories sprung up, not conflicting with Einstein's equations, but augmenting and refining them. Still, no one knew for sure. Frank only knew that when the ship went, he went with it. If that meant now, so be it.

The tunnel was dark, but when it opened up into the

ship hangar, Frank squinted to see in the bright lights. His eyes adjusted, and he looked at The Terran. It resembled an airplane, just slightly, with a retractable pair of wings growing from the sides. In the event they made it to an atmosphere and were to attempt a landing, these wings would control their flight. Alien atmospheres could bring any unforeseen problem, and no one knew if Earth-style wings would ever be needed, or useful, but the scientists agreed that using Earth's current scientific knowledge and common sense increased the chances for survival. How different than the first spacecraft from Earth: The *Apollo* rockets, little more than missiles, and their lunar landers, almost random in their shape; the *Viking* lander, asymmetrical and gangly; the *Challenger* ships to the outer planets, conglomerations of mechanical parts. The Terran looked closer to the old *Space Shuttle* design, though longer, sleeker. It was their work, all of them, which made this project possible - those long, tedious years of perfecting space flight and the reusable craft, learning about controlled reentry, understanding that death just a mile from earth is as final as death thirty light years away.

Terran had her wings retracted to less than a third of its span, giving it the look of a jet. The fuselage, a hundred yards long and half that wide, gleamed yellow in the artificial light of the hangar. Frank had never seen it anywhere else. Still, the body was far from smooth. All over were doors, some opened with instruments sticking out, others closed, waiting for the call to duty. In the emptiness of space where friction was not a problem, these devices could be extended and put to their tasks, then pulled back should the ship need to reduce wind resistance and better control her path. That was the marvel of this design, the adaptability. Most people had never seen it, and unless the crew returned successfully, they never would. Frank smiled to himself. Actually, most of the people alive, maybe all of them, will have died of all age long before this ship could return.

Mick stopped and grabbed his hand. "This is where I get off, Frank. You are the last to arrive. The danger was too great to have you here any sooner than necessary. Your crew is aboard, and the countdown will start as soon as you join them." The man smiled and shook Sorrel's hand vigorously. "I wish I was going with you."

Frank Sorrel started up the steps toward the ship entrance. This was all happening so differently than he expected!

But moments later he stood aboard The Terran, on the bridge. He wore a light headset and spoke confidently.

"Armstrong control, this is our final radio check. How do you read?"

"Loud and clear, Commander. Are you ready for final countdown?"

Sorrel looked around the bridge, noting the officers at their stations.

Tamela Zhan stood at the navigation console. She was young and pretty, but strong. She read the power output readouts, and said, half-jokingly, "Let's get out of here before I change my mind."

At the science station Hal Ramage said, "Ready here, sir." Ramage was a career military man, about 40 years old.

Gerald Hannah, the replacement pilot, crawled out from underneath his work station. A large man, maybe 35 years old, Sorrel thought he was more the athlete-type than pilot. "As soon as I replace this suspect panel coupling, I'll be ready. It'll only be two minutes." Sorrel was nervous working with someone so completely new, but the choice was not in his hands.

Sorrel spoke into the headset. "Mission control, we're almost ready. First office Lane is having a cargo problem."

"Yes, we know. Her gear was mislaid and certain personal items are unaccounted for. It's probably on board, but you'll have to find it after launch. We are commencing final countdown. Launch in five minutes."

At that moment the door leading to the bridge flew open, sliding furiously against its mechanisms with the help of Regina Lane.

"Of all the dumb-ass moves! If that cargo geek lost my

stuff I'll rip his nuts off!" Lane was 28, short but well-built, Sorrel decided. She was good-looking, but right now she wasn't looking pleasant.

"I'm sorry 'bout your gear, Regina, but it's not considered essential material --"

"Maybe not to you, Sorrel! But if I'm going out on a three-month exploration I'd better have my things!" Despite the importance she placed on her possessions, Regina Lane began strapping in for the launch.

Hal Ramage wore a lecherous grin. "I'll loan you anything you need, Regina. Come to my quarters and we'll --"

She spun and jabbed her finger an inch from Ramage's face. Sorrel felt sure she had considered grabbing his neck. "You watch it, Ramage! Allowing informal bridge conversation doesn't mean you can be insulting to me!"

Sorrel stepped between them. "Get back to your work, both of you. Hal, you're out of line. Regina, get your mind on your work and we'll find your gear in a while if it's on the ship." *Three months!* He wondered what even the next three days would bring. He returned his attention to the headset. "Mission control, this is Terran. Confirm that we are ready for final launch countdown. Get us out of here."

Four and a half minutes later, just seconds before the launch, the bubble above them retracted and for the first time The Terran was aimed at the stars.

***

The launch itself had been exciting, but uneventful. Gerald Hannah leaned back in his chair. "For every minute of excitement in space travel there are 24 hours of total boredom. We have hyperlight speed and are on course for the Cygnus VII system. Nothing happens for about two days. I really need to catch up on the ship mission reports, so I'll take the first watch if that's okay."

"Okay, Gerald." Sorrel agreed. "I'll see you in six hours. C'mon Regina. Lets go look for your gear in cargo."

Regina Lane followed Frank through one of the two doors which led down the length of the ship. Tamela Zhan and Hal Ramage left through the other, down a parallel corridor. When Hannah was certain they had left he flipped the switch on his communications console.

"Mission Control. Garret, this is Hannah."

"Go ahead, Hannah. We're on closed channel."

"I don't like it, Garret. The military will have our heads when they find out we're experimenting on their engines without even informing their officers."

"They won't find out." the other voice said firmly. "At least, not until we have enough feedback to show it as a success. We've been over this before. The military would just take over the project, and use it to shore up their power base. This time, let them ask for *our* help."

"But these people deserve to know the risk. If something goes wrong, what then?"

"Don't let anything go wrong. Just tell me, Hannah -- are you going ahead with the plan?"

"Yes, damn you!" he shouted. Then more softly as he pounded the switch off. "I'll do it."

In the small cargo hold near the back of the ship Sorrel and Regina Lane continued searching through the hastily-stored materials looking for her missing pack. Sorrel already sensed that something was seriously wrong, but she refused to talk about specifics, and he was hesitant to push the issue this early in the flight. He moved boxes and equipment aside, but Lane tossed sensitive equipment around in a frantic search. Sorrel stopped.

"I don't think we're going to find it. Probably we all had something left behind. I haven't even checked my stuff over. Whatever it is, I'm sure we'll all be able to help you get what you need to get by."

Frustrated but calm, Regina lane replied, "Nobody has what I need; I have to keep looking."

Sorrel didn't continue the search. To exert too much power now could cause problems later on, at times when they may rely on one another for survival or sanity, but obviously Lane was being deceptively silent.

"Regina," he tried, "What's going on?"

"I need my stuff."

He stood, arms folded. "Lieutenant Commander Lane, stand at attention."

She looked out of the corner of her eye. She hadn't expected Frank Sorrel to conduct affairs in such an official manner, but this was the second time he had done just that. She hesitated, not yet sure how far she could push him.

"Attention! Now!" His voice was no louder, but certainly more forceful. She stood at attention, but her face remained lost in thought. "Lieutenant Commander Lane, it has become apparent that you have brought aboard this ship, or attempted to bring aboard, an item or items which are not approved for this voyage. Is that true?"

She stared ahead, silently, the smallest tear welling up in one eye.

"Regina, look," he said more softly, "I don't want to be a hard ass, but this is going to be a long voyage. You're an officer, and you know how hard it is to maintain any kind of discipline on a trip like this; We'll be light years away from any military court, any other source of authority. I can't afford to let anyone break ship policy, no matter how small the violation or who makes it. What did you bring?"

Lane looked down, talking just above a whisper. "Metrocycline."

"Metrocycline?" he repeated, confused. "But why? That's only used to treat --" he stopped talking, and by reflex stepped back.

She looked at him, anger in her eyes. "You don't need to run. Brangan's disease is not contagious. I'll die, but no one else will."

"How did you get past the medical scans?"

"I didn't. But the doctor who certified me was happier to flirt with me than to concentrate on my medical problems. The scans picked it up, but I was able to distract him enough

23

that he didn't see the indications. Afterwards it was easier for him to certify me rather than repeat the scans. No one knows."

"I see." Frank understood how easy it would be for someone like Regina Lane to overpower some young doctor's concentration. He understood, also, why she wanted it hidden. Brangan's disease was fatal, and no cure was known. Metrocycline would keep her functioning while the illness took its course. She wanted to die in space rather than on earth. He didn't know her specific reasons, but he imagined that he would share them if he was the one dying.

"What happens now, Commander?" she said.

"We'll talk about it -- after we find your Metrocycline." He headed for the door. "Now that we know what we're looking for, the Medlab scanners will pinpoint where it is on the ship."

"If it's here," she added.

Sorrel was already on his way down the corridor.

On the bridge Gerald Hannah activated security locks on the two doors. Normally it wouldn't keep out members of the crew, but he reworked the mechanisms so it would appear like a door malfunction. If anyone noticed something out of the ordinary, by time they made it through the door his work would be done. Then it didn't matter. He still had hours before Sorrel planned to relieve him on watch, so there was no particular hurry. He had some personal business to take care of. Hannah plugged a communications module into the board. This was a simple data container, capable of holding thirty gigabytes of information. His message was simpler, though. He spoke slowly into the recording device.

"It's wrong for the military to control our knowledge of space. Especially these vessels which are for exploration; they need to have the information open to all people. My part in this experiment is motivated by the desire to see scientific advances made without a new weapon being the automatic result.

"The rest of this message is for my love Traci:

"To have you in my life I would do most anything. But

24

I have respected you too much to try. This new mission is the only option I have left. Staying on Earth, or on the moon, means a chance of accidentally running into you. You want me out of your life completely. I want you so badly, yet more than that I want you to be happy. So I won't be on Earth - ever again.

"There's so much more to say than this message, but I'm on another course now. I love you, Traci. I miss you."

Hannah transmitted the message on an open channel to Mission Control.

He stopped briefly at the main viewscreen. Hyperlight travel created an odd kaleidoscope of images on the screen as the ship moved faster than the light ahead of them. Stars swirled and coalesced toward the center of the screen, always giving the illusion that the ship was colliding with them. The computers compensated somewhat for the effect, giving a more understandable representation of what was ahead, but Hannah didn't worry any more about what he saw. He removed a small box from his pocket, a device no larger than a pack of cigarettes, but something that existed nowhere else in the world. The box was black and featureless except for a connecting module at one end, and this he plugged into the main engine console. At least if it doesn't work, he thought, probably no one will live long enough to care. Then he returned to his chair, strapped himself in, and closed his eyes. Screwing up courage he wasn't sure he had, Gerald Hannah opened his eyes and punched one button.

***

Inside Tamela Zhan's cabin, Hal Ramage sat leafing through a magazine. He wasn't really reading it, but didn't care to admit that the beginning of the flight -- the real flight, not some simulation -- had him quite scared. Across the room Tamela Zhan began taking off her uniform.

"Do you think anyone suspects about us?" she said.

"I don't see how they could; I haven't said three words

25

to you during the entire flight simulation process. I've been rude and lecherous toward Lane, but haven't paid much attention to you at all. No one knows a thing."

"I hope you're right."

He stood up and walked over to her. She was beautiful, and his attraction to her was immediate. They met after each had been selected for the flight, and their time together was always brief and full of danger. He liked that.

Besides," he said. "We're here now. If they had found out that we were lovers on the moon, one or both of us would have been kicked out on their ass, but there's no way they're going to turn this ship around now, not on a matter of policy." He kissed her neck and ran his hands down her back.

Tamela Zhan shivered at the touch. "You know," she whispered. "It might not be a good idea to get Regina so pissed off at you. She might not be your favorite person, but she is second in command."

Ramage pulled her toward him. "Screw her."

"I've got a better idea," she cooed, falling into his arms.

***

Frank Sorrel reached the Medlab. This mission could have started better, he thought. Regina often was a bitch, but if she's battling Brangan's disease, I can see why her personality has been so grim. Finding the chemical scanner, Sorrel linked it with the main computer and directed the ship's sensor to begin looking for the correct combination of chemicals. The search should only take a few minutes. The Metrocycline couldn't save Regina Lane from the ultimate effects of the malady, but without the drug she would soon degenerate into a pain-racked, incoherent madwoman. Sorrel had seen Brangan's patients before, mostly on Mars where it was first discovered. Many people committed suicide when they found out they had Brangan's, rather than face the deterioration of their mind and body. Regina had chosen to take this mission, to stave off the effects as long as possible. What would she

26

ultimately do out here?

Sorrel read the screen:

NO METROCYCLINE WITHIN SCANNER RANGE

None. Sorrel felt certain they didn't have the resources to synthesize such a complex chemical. Lane had three or fours days, maybe, before the best they could do for her would be sedation and restraints. He thought about the possibility of turning the ship around, but to decelerate from hyperlight was infinitely slower than accelerating. By time they even began the trip home Regina Lane would be dead.

Suddenly the ship lurched forward. Sorrel knew the ship as well as anyone could. He knew he should not feel acceleration in the vacuum of space. He knew the ship should not be accelerating now anyway. After the initial pull of the ship Sorrel expected to be hurled by whatever malfunction had just occurred and smashed into the opposite wall by the incredible force of hyperlight gravity. He was happy not to have his bones shattered to powder, but that it didn't happen when it should have filled him with a different kind of fear. He shot to the door and as he nearly flew down the corridor toward the bridge he met Regina Lane, who also ran urgently toward the control center of the ship.

"What the hell is going on?" She yelled.

"No idea!" he blurted as he passed her and reached the doorway to the bridge.

***

Unable to differentiate between lurchings of the ship and their own movements, Tamela Zhan and Hal Ramage were unaware of the danger. They reached the climax of their efforts when it struck.

***

The door didn't open. Lane caught up with him quickly. "Who's in there?" She tried the door override system, but it would not yield.

"It should just be Hannah. Zhan and Ramage left the same time we did. I don't know where they went, and they could have come back." He tried disconnecting the entire touchpad controls for the doorway, but it wouldn't work.

Lane pounded on the door. "Open the door, Hannah, you son of a bitch!"

"It's soundproof, Regina. Besides, whatever's going on had to be planned. That movement of the ship was something I'd never heard of before in hyperlight. And this door being locked is no coincidence. Plus this Hannah guy being added at the last minute? I should have known better."

The ship lurched again send Lane and Sorrel off balance and falling toward the floor. Their eyes met briefly, but in that instant *time stopped*.

***

"Garret! Come in, Garret! We're accelerating too fast! What do I do? Garret!" Hannah moved frantically about the bridge. He disconnected the box he had smuggled on board, but the ship continued to act on its own. He shut down switches all over the room, but everything seemed to be locked in the activated position. On the viewscreen the strange dance of the stars had quickened, tenfold or more. They appeared at the edges of the screen and disappeared into the center swirls almost immediately. Hannah returned to the communications panel.

"Garret -- I can't abort the experiment! We're hurtling out of control and the second stage is about to kick in. How do I --"

The second stage knocked him into the Comm chair. He was facing the viewport when all movement stopped. He stopped breathing, his heart was not beating, blood flow halted. All was silent. For an instant he felt he was dying. This, he figured, was the sensation of the ending of life. But his mind kept working, and the lights in front of him kept moving. Light and thought were alone. He tried to move his eyes, but he couldn't even feel his own body.

The stars flew by more quickly. After a time (though he couldn't measure time and only knew that other thoughts had past) the stars became a blur. Then the screen went black. The room around him had darkened, but he had no vision other than where his eyes were transfixed. Then something new appeared at the edge of the screen, and though it was distorted and quickly became a lone dot in the center of the screen, Hannah saw that it was a galaxy. A galaxy! Then another appeared and disappeared - and another, only more quickly. Soon even the galaxies were becoming a blur.

Unable to move but aware of what occurred in front of him, Hannah felt his sanity slipping away. He lost it completely as he watched the last galaxy fly by.

***

The brains of Tamela Zhan and Hal Ramage didn't experience the same thought processes as Gerald Hannah. Their bodies became one electrical charge as they responded to the meeting of their climax with the second wave. For a short time it was ecstasy, but then it became an agony.

***

Frank Sorrel looked at Regina Lane's right eye, which was trained on his. In the first subjective moments after time stopped he tried to understand what was happening. The Terran was accelerating - at least, that was his guess based on the feelings he had. *Had Hannah made an error? Not likely, or the door wouldn't have been locked this way. How fast were they going? Why couldn't he feel, but he could see? The phenomenon of stopping time was science-fiction, but he knew it had because he wasn't breathing, yet he was alive. Or was he?*

Regina was not moving either. *Had they even hit the*

29

floor? His peripheral vision was poor. All he could see clearly was her one eye, about four feet away.

She was going to die soon. Perhaps they all would; Very probably in fact. But for her it was a certainly. She doesn't know yet that the Metrocycline is not on the ship. He noticed, he thought, a softness in her eyes, one he had never noticed before. Doubtful anyone had, because she wouldn't allow it.

Because weak women don't succeed.

That thought was not his!

Regina!

Frank, why are we frozen like this?

I don't know, exactly. We have accelerated, probably to a tremendous speed. That was the lurching we both felt. Apparently it's fast enough to stop our normal sensation of time.

But we can think, and see.

Yes. That means time isn't fully stopped, because light impulses can travel, and brain waves, which travel at the speed of light, can operate. Whatever happened, it somehow ruptured or penetrated the hyperlight warp bubble of the ship to have this effect. I'm not sure why we can read each others thoughts, though.

I think I do. Brain waves are not very strong; in reality they're nothing more than weak radio waves. But here, there's nothing to stop the free travel of brain waves - no chemical activity, no blood flowing through the body, not even atomic vibrations. You've heard it said that there's no resistance to thought in a void? Well, this must be it. Our thoughts travel freely between one another because there isn't anything, even the smallest barrier, to stop them. As long as we can think, we can communicate.

I wonder how long that will be.

Probably at least long enough for us to hate each other. Right now we're very conscious of our thoughts, guarding them carefully. Eventually, though, we'll be unable to control them, to prevent random thoughts from getting out. The mind will often think terrible things, just because it can -

even ideas or actions that the person would never consciously consider or condone. The mind, though, will allow the concept in. If we're here long we will read very ugly thoughts from one another. Some might be real, but most will be the fabrication of a renegade brain. The problem is that the other person won't know which is which. We'll go crazy, or if we survive build up such a hatred for each other that when this ends we'll try to kill each other, or ourselves, or both.

You're assuming that our minds will get fatigued enough that we necessarily let our guard down. We don't know that this will happen, that our minds will tire. Without time can there really be fatigue?

Time is not completely stopped, like you said. If it were, light and electromagnetic forces would not operate. It may come slowly, but fatigue will come. It could take what would seem to us to be days or weeks, or even months -- that's if we don't disintegrate because of what's happening out there. And if we're like this very long.

Odds are that there's nothing in space to stop us until whatever is happening ceases. Space is mostly a lot of nothing.

That's okay.

Why do you say that?

Because I picked up your thoughts quickly enough to know there's no Metrocycline on the ship. If we don't blow up or crash I'll die in a few days anyway.

***

Tamela Zhan and Hal Ramage continued in their electrostatic agony. Gerald Hannah had thoughts, but they were incomprehensible, even to himself.

***

The capacity of the human mind is nearly limitless, and it only the sense of disbelief that keeps us from taking greater advantage of the knowledge we have. Through their mental link, Sorrel and Lane talked, touching on issues they would never have dreamed of in their conscious state, what they had come to call 'active' life. But even without the usual limits certain questions came up again and again.

Frank, how long do you think it has been?

Our thoughts could be passing between us instantaneously, or almost so. If time has not fully stopped then we could expect to eventually shift position. Though I cannot feel my body I don't think I have moved, and you don't appear to have moved either. The conversations we have would take weeks or even months in normal life, but I would not be surprised to find that only a fraction of a second of real time has passed.

Do you hate me yet?

No. I love you.

I don't think you could really love me, though I have held the same types of feelings for you. You just feel connected to me because we've shared this situation and talked non-stop for so long. That's not love.

Why not, Regina?

Because we would not have this connection if things were normal.

I wouldn't have been able to get to know you, because you wouldn't have let me. Here you had no choice but to open up a bit. A certain measure of love is simply familiarity; it's like that for everyone. But people become familiar with one another, maybe even more than you and I have become through this time, and they don't automatically fall in love. We've seen the good and the bad in each other. There are things about you I don't like, and maybe if things were different those things would never be discussed the way we have discussed them. But I have also seen the good parts of you, as I see them, and I have seen the real you. We couldn't pretend much here, you know. You had to open up. So did I. You did, and I know you, and I love you.

I'd rather you didn't.

Because of Brangan's disease?

Of course.

Anything can happen.

32

Right. What do you think is happening with the others?

Sorrel saw Lane blink. In the same instant his body slumped to the floor and he lost consciousness.

***

He awoke, afraid to move, the pain in his head screaming for stillness. He glanced over to Lane, but she was gone. He shot to his feet, and then fell over. More slowly, he rose. The door to the bridge remained closed and locked, so he made his way toward the crew's quarters. He stopped when he saw the light on in the Medlab.

Lane was standing over Tamela Zhan and Hal Ramage, each lying on examination tables. Both were naked, with severe burn marks across their bodies. Lane studied the readouts from her hand scanner, merely glancing up for a second when Sorrell entered the room.

"I think they'll both live, but Ramage will be a long time in recovery. He took the worst"

"What happened to them?"

She didn't look up. "Whereas you and I communicated quite well from two yards away while we were frozen, these two were already communicating -- physically -- when the phenomenon occurred. It apparently created a sort of electrostatic overload. The burns are mostly first and second degree, but both needed CPR to get going again."

"Then you weren't unconscious very long after the effect ended?"

"I guess not, or I wouldn't have been able to revive them. I don't know for sure. I woke up about fifteen minutes ago, and I guess they're just lucky that the medical officer was the first one here."

"We need to get into the bridge as soon as possible," he said. "Can you leave them? How long before they are conscious, or mobile?"

"I'm going to keep them sedated for a while. Physically, they'll be laid up for about a week, maybe longer

33

for Ramage because his injuries seem more severe. I wonder what has happened to their minds. The electrostatic overload lasted the entire duration of the phenomenon. How long that was, in real time, is anyone's guess, but if they were conscious there's a possibility that their minds are seriously affected, damaged, if not destroyed." She gave each a nutrient injection. "I'm free for whatever you need."

Sorrel head back toward the doorway. "I'm going to get a torch and open a hole to get into the bridge. You check life support and see if we have anything to worry about."

"I'm on my way."

Burning through the bulkhead required extra oxygen from the air, so Sorrel waited until Lane returned to tell him that the life support was fully operational before he started to cut through. The life support system, operated by an atomic battery rather than ships power to protect against engine power failures, showed a .5% drop in power Levels. The battery was designed to last a year, so they surmised that their launch took place about two days ago. Sorrel still believed that whatever had happened to them it had something to do with speed. The lurch of the ship, the seemingly impossible stoppage of time, these were all unknown events, but he recalled lectures and theories from his earlier days of space training which gave his cause to wonder if they had reached a new limit of velocity. Hopefully when they entered the bridge they could get a bearing on their position and find out for sure.

Regina would survive for a few days without the Metrocycline. She was very calm, amazingly so. He had shared some intimate thoughts with her over the time of the effect, but now she was reluctant even to talk, or look at him. He couldn't understand her situation, not really, knowing that she would only be alive for a couple days, no matter what. Of course, depending on where they were, the others might have just slightly more time.

He was nearly through when Lane said, "Why did you cut out the entire door? You could have been through quicker with just a crawlspace."

34

"Yes, but then every time we wanted to move on and off the bridge, we might have to crawl through or just cut a bigger hole. If the door is permanently damaged I want to have better access than that. Just seemed easier to do it now."

"You're an optimist to think that it matters," she said, looking at the floor.

"You went to the trouble of saving Zhan and Ramage," he replied. "You must think there's some chance, too."

Sorrel made a final pass with the torch and pushed the metal slab over. They stepped in quickly. The bridge was still. On all stations except the independent life support, there were no indications of power or activity on the ship. Lighting ran through the atomic batteries also, otherwise they would be in total darkness. Lane was the first to notice the figure of Gerald Hannah sitting at the main navigational chair. The two officers walked around to the front, standing between Hannah and the black screen at the bow of the ship. Hannah, eyes opened, stared through them at the screen. His eyes were dry and red. He didn't blink. "Is he alive?" Sorrel asked. Lane pulled out her scanner.

"He's alive, but I'm not reading anything but minimal brain activity."

"What do you mean minimal?"

"I mean, there's barely enough activity to keep his body functioning, but no other brain wave activity. It's strange. He's not in a coma, but he's not merely unconscious. I would have to do more testing, but if I'm reading this right, he has effectively switched off. His mind is a blank."

She took a pocket light and shined the bright light in one of Hannah's eyes, but got no reaction. "I don't think the light impulses are even getting to the brain. It's as if he simply turned himself off. I've never seen anything like it."

Sorrel talked while looking at the other ship consoles, looking for some indicator of power. "Regina, how long did that effect seem like to us? We know it was just a couple days, but if we had found out it was weeks or even months, would you have been surprised?"

35

"No."

"Right, and that means Hannah experienced the same time sense we did. If he was sitting in the position he is now, looking at the screen, when this started it means he spent the entire time just that way. No one to communicate with, unlike us. No electrostatic activity like the others. Nothing. Unable to move, unable to do anything but stare at the screen. Was it operating? Was it blank? Whether he lost his mind because of what he saw on the screen or because he spent all that time with only his own thoughts, I don't know. But I can see where he would have to go mad, stuck with only his own fears to keep him company."

"And maybe his guilt," Lane added.

"Yes, you could be right. " Sorrel left the staring figure of Gerald Hannah and moved to the main engineering station. His knowledge of the systems were adequate, but even the best experts couldn't help them right now. "Can we divert enough energy from life support to the ships systems to get a readout on our situation? We have enough power reserve there." He almost said more than we need, but he checked himself. The situation was grim, but he couldn't bring himself to think it was hopeless.

"I'm on it," Lane answered. Within seconds the bridge lit up with the activity of a dozen panels and hundreds of small lights. Sorrel was relieved to see them on again. The ship had seemed too much like a tomb without the comfort of the colored lights.

"How about turning the screen on? Can we get a visual so we can find out where the Hell we are?'

Lane checked the panel in front of her, and looked up at the blank surface in front of them. She looked down again, and when her eyes rose to meet Sorrel's for the first time since they regained movement her expression was simply astonishment.

"Frank, It's on."

There was no light coming through the screen. There were no planets, no stars, nothing. "That's impossible," he said. "Check your instruments, Regina. There isn't anywhere

36

in the universe where you cannot find stars. There's no position, no orientation that would account for it."

He stepped over to the console and manipulated the controls. Everything said that the screen was on, that whatever was outside the ship could be seen inside. "I'm sending out a probe." He set the launch and three seconds later they saw a very small flash on the viewscreen as the probe ignited its small engines and flew ahead. It disappeared a few seconds later into the void.

"I saw that," Lane said. "Everything's working perfectly, isn't it?"

"Yes. Somehow -- we've left the known universe."

At that moment a sound reached them from the doorway. Both spun instantly to see the naked figures of Tamela Zhan and Hal Ramage. Neither had burns.

***

They took the body of Gerald Hannah to Sickbay, and monitored his life signs. Sorrel considered it a waste of time and energy because without a mind, could Hannah ever be truly alive again? But the others felt it was the right thing to do, and Frank Sorrel saw little real harm. They convened in the small conference room, little more than an alcove ten foot square with a table and five chairs. A smaller version of the viewscreen rested on the wall just above their line of sight. It was on, but no one looked at it. Zhan and Ramage had returned to their uniforms, appearing none the worse for wear. Frank Sorrel stood, holding tightly to the back of his chair.

"How are they, really, Regina?"

"I've given them every test I can think of -- scanning, at least. Both are extremely sensitive to touch. Even proximity with another person seems to be very painful. Other than that, and an increased activity in certain parts of their brain they seem fine."

Zhan said, "What about Hannah? We managed to come out of it okay. Any chance that he will, too?'

"Unlikely," Ramage said. "Our problems were physical in nature. I have a feeling his was mostly mental. Have we managed to get any information at all about where we are and why we can't see anything outside the ship?"

Sorrel walked about the table. "There doesn't appear to be anything wrong with the ship sensors. As far as we can tell, there just isn't anything to grab on to. Nothing for the sensors to pick up."

"What about a black hole?" Ramage said. "Could we have entered one of those?"

"Nothing we know supports being able to remain alive inside a black hole," Lane answered. Evidence suggests that entering a black hole, while possible theoretically, would certainly end life. No, I don't think that's the answer. The ship engineering logs are incomplete, but we engaged an engine formula that had never been attempted before. I think Hannah programmed it into the computer just after take-off."

"So he did this intentionally?" Zhan said.

Sorrel said "He was added to the ship's compliment at the last minute. It's a good bet that he was added for that reason. The military, or someone, wanted to test something new but was afraid of leaking information about it -- or of something going wrong -- I don't know. But we accelerated far past the point the logs could record. We reached a speed at least 100 times hyperlight speed."

"That's impossible!" Zhan exclaimed.

"It's happened," Lane came back, a hint of disgust in her voice. She didn't like other women, and Tamela Zhan particularly so. Sorrel had noticed it in their pre-flight simulations.

"Yes, it has happened." Sorrell confirmed. "We could easily have traveled outside the boundaries of our universe. We have no frame of reference in any direction, but that in itself suggests that this is exactly what happened. The question now: What do we do about it?'

Lane broke in. "We don't have enough power to turn around and go back. All we have is life support atomic

38

batteries. Using them to power the ship will drain them quickly. We have roughly six months of power left, powering the necessary ship's operations beyond life support, but any attempt to use it for navigation or other significant drains could take it to nothing in hours."

"We can't just sit here," Ramage said. "I'll take the chance of not getting back, but I can't accept not trying."

"Actually, we're probably not sitting at all," Sorrel said. "If the theory is right and we left the known universe due to our speed, we are most likely still traveling at a very high rate of speed, possibly many hundreds of times the speed of light. Trouble is, without anything to use as a frame of reference there's no way to tell. The ship's power was a combination of solid fuel, atomics, and using the gravitational pull of stellar objects to propel the ship past lightspeed. We don't know when the engines ran out of power, or which of the three sources gave out first, but the momentum is probably still moving us. I doubt we have enough power in the life support batteries to slow us down, let alone stop us and turn us around."

The room remained silent for a long time as each of them tried to understand what had happened and come to grips with their fate. Tamela Zhan spoke first.

"Then there isn't anything to do but die when life support runs out."

"Wait a minute," Ramage snapped. "If we left the universe, where are we? I mean, no one really knew what would be out here, but I've heard every theory from a vast emptiness, to Heaven, to a barrier where existence ended. I don't know what is out here, but I can't believe that we wouldn't find anything at all. Maybe matter is few and far between, and maybe my puny human mind can't really comprehend what we're dealing with, but there must be something out here. I say we look for it."

They agreed that their survival could be completely out of their control, but that they wouldn't give in to death as long as there was any hope. It was even suggested that maybe death would not find them way out here. Frank Sorrel looked at Regina, who didn't return the glance. But both knew they would soon find out if death held any power outside the universe.

***

Although the clock kept record of time that had passed, Regina Lane stifled a sarcastic laugh whenever she looked at it. Why measure time when you have no purpose in knowing day, night, today or tomorrow? Of course, the practical function onboard was to keep a duty schedule on the bridge. One person remained constantly on duty and aware, watching the sensors and the viewscreen for signs of....well, anything. Her shift was nearly over, one hour of eight remaining, then she would be free for a full 24 hours – she couldn't bring herself to call it a day – until once more she looked at lifeless consoles and pointless screens. She had filled eighteen shifts already. It would kill a few minutes to figure out how many days that worked out to be, but she didn't really want to know.

Her Brangan's seemed to be in remission. On Earth by now she would have been a babbling idiot, little more than a drooling vegetable. Mediscans showed the virus remained in her body, but inactive. Despite the hopelessness of the situation this was good news. Death didn't scare her, but she wanted to face it aware and alert, not feeble and helpless. Sorrell suggested that a catalyst in Earth's atmosphere which activated the virus was missing from the filtered, scrubbed and thrice-cleaned air of The Terran. Apparently, Lane had mused, she would live long enough to die. Sorrell berated her for that attitude. No matter what, he wouldn't surrender to despair. Though she hadn't known him well, prior to the flight she regarded him as somewhat pessimistic. As they shared thoughts during the time stoppage, she learned that he had no regrets about leaving Earth behind, that he was escaping a world he didn't understand. Yet, here in the vast wasteland, this incredible nothing, he seemed optimistic, hopeful.

A small flash of light reached the corner of her eye. She turned to the console, but there was nothing there.

Ramage was due soon. He spent almost every minute in his quarters, alone, as did Tamela Zhan. Since their experience during the accident, day by day contact with the others – especially each other – became harder and harder to bear. Even being in the room together caused them physical pain. She suspected for a while that either of them could become homicidal, but neither could get close enough to another person to inflict real damage, now that the rifles and other weapons were locked away.

The light caught her eye again, only this time it remained on as she turned to face it. A faint blue light on the sensor grid indicated that something, somewhere, was being detected. For a moment she stood frozen, uncertain what to do, since in all the days nothing had happened to warrant doing anything. Finally she hit the communications panel.

"Everybody get up here – we've found something!"

From a dead sleep Sorrell arrived in less than 30 seconds. Ramage walked slowly in a few minutes later and stood off in the far corner of the room, partially behind a sleeping communications panel. Tamela Zhan appeared a few minutes later, interested but unwilling to come closer than three or four feet from Sorrell or Lane.

"What is it?" Zhan asked.

Sorrell forced a smile. Those were the first words she had spoken in days. "Way too soon to tell, but there is definitely something ahead of us. The sensors can't get a lock on how big or how far away it is. It's either something small nearby, or something very big but very far away."

Lane stared at the screen, which still showed nothing. "What is the range of our sensor grid? I still don't see anything."

"With absolutely nothing to deflect the light being collected, nothing to distort the data, the range is virtually limitless."

Zhan countered. "It has limits, or we would have

detected this before."

"Point made," Sorrell admitted. "If the range had no limits anything that is there now would have been there before. So all we know so far is that something is ahead. In about four minutes we'll know a little more. We'll know if we are getting closer to it, and something about its size."

The next four minutes passed in complete silence. Sorrell, for his part, simply didn't want to speculate. The others? He couldn't imagine what would be going through their minds. As the new readings were collected and evaluated by the computer, Sorrell pumped his fist in the air.

"Hot damn!" he said. "According to the readings we are approaching the object at many times the speed of light, and accelerating toward it."

"Toward what?" Lane demanded, peering over his shoulder.

"Either one object larger than a billion billion galaxies, or it's a billion billion galaxies."

***

It was over an hour before Sorrell wanted to really say more. He, Lane and Zhan stood together on the bridge. Ramage had returned to his quarters, wordlessly. Zhan still kept her distance, but seemed a little more comfortable being in a room with others than she was before.

"There's no doubt about it, then," she said. "We're heading back into the universe?"

Lane continued to look at the blank screen. "Well, we're heading toward an immensely large cluster of galaxies, that's for sure. But is it the universe? Is it *our* universe? And besides, if we're accelerating toward it, it won't matter."

"Why not?" Lane asked.

"Because we were going fast enough to leave one universe, and we're going even faster now. We'll pass it by."

"I don't think so," Sorrell said. "At one point we were going so fast that even time itself was slowed down. We decelerated after that, and our acceleration is probably only recent, due to the infinitesimal gravitational attraction of the upcoming universe from this distance. Who knows what speed we were reduced to at one point. It may have been close to nothing or it may have always been faster than light, and increased as we glided a bit closer to the universe ahead. We'll pick up speed, but once we reach the universe the different gravitational attractions will slow us down again. At some point we will probably go sublight, and may even be able to maneuver."

"Maneuver to where?" Zhan snapped. "That's not *our* universe, not unless we turned around, and you said there was not enough power for that. There's nothing out there for us. What if, by some amazing stroke of fate, we can maneuver. Where would we go in a universe that probably doesn't even obey the same laws of physics we know?"

Ramage's voice came over the communication panel. His voice was deadpan and emotionless. "Space is curved."

It took a moment, but Regina Lane finally understood.

"That is our universe! Don't you see, Hal is right. If we accept the notion that space is curved, there's no reason we could not have traveled around the fabric of space, and we're approaching the universe from the other side." Sorrell whistled.

"Don't get your hopes up," Ramage added in the same monotone. "You'll never even find your galaxy, let alone be able to maneuver to it. And even if you did, it's not the same one you left."

Sorrell frowned. "He right, again. The odds of even locating the Milky Way galaxy is astronomical. The only reason we can even talk about this is that none of us can fathom the sheer immensity of the universe. If we understood it we couldn't handle it. But finding it even through the greatest miracle ever known, being able to work our way to it using only our momentum – which is all we have left – is unthinkable."

Lane asked, "What does he mean it's not the same one

43

we left."

"He means," Zhan answered, "that because of relativity and our speed, so much time has passed, perhaps millions of years or hundreds of millions, that the galaxy isn't even the same shape it was before. The universe has expanded – which will help to make sure we don't shoot out the other side no matter what our speed – and the galaxy has rotated, the Earth has long ago turned to dust or fallen into the sun, and the sun itself is possibly gone. There's no way to calculate the time that has passed, but its more than a safe bet that everything we ever knew is gone."

No one spoke for a moment, then the silence was demolished by a scream from Regina Lane. Her face was frozen in terror, her gaze at the viewscreen. As all three watched, a small figure in one of their spacesuits moved slowly in front of the screen, pushed itself away from the ship, and began drifting away, becoming smaller almost immediately.

Sorrell ran to the communications panel. "Ramage! Ramage, what are you doing? Use the thrusters in your suit to move back toward the ship before it's too late! Ramage!"

Zhan didn't move, but she turned toward Sorrell. "He won't have his communications open. He doesn't want to hear you, or anyone. He wants to be alone now. Once we started moving back toward something, he couldn't stand the thought of once more being surrounded by everything, literally everything. He hated being confined by the ship, close to us. He went out to be alone. In a few minutes, once he has experienced the solitude, he'll open up his suit, so even that will not confine him."

Lane walked toward Zhan, but the second woman backed up a step. "Did he tell you all this?"

"No. But I knew. I thought about doing it myself. It's hard not to, even now."

***

The first speck of light didn't appear for almost two weeks. Tamela Zhan no longer suffered from the desire to throw herself out an airlock, though she remained alone most of the time and never came close enough that a touch would be possible. Regina and Sorrell worked together, trying to make a plan. They consulted Zhan, but respected her inability to interact with others. Likely, they confided, she would never be right again.

Despite all their plans, their theories, and their hopes, what would occur as they entered this universe would be only a matter of luck. Their power was so weak that they couldn't affect any change in their trajectory. That wasn't strictly true. If they started making a move now, slight though it would be, the angle would be multiplied over the vast distances. But what was the point of moving when you were too far away to know what to move toward? Once they knew, it would be too late. What small amount of power they had would be used for that incredibly unlikely possibility of a landing. The universe, however inconceivably big, is still mostly space, so their chances of even coming within a hundred light-years of a galaxy was unbelievably remote. Then, if they did, the chances of coming within striking distance of a planetary system was again so remote as to be virtually impossible. And then, even if they did, the chances that the planet they found would support life, or that they could land the ship, were outrageous. Still, they planned, because there was nothing else to do.

The first galaxy passed by slowly, and Sorrell estimated it was over a hundred million light years away. Over the next few weeks more lumbered by, and the screen began to fill with remote and almost imperceptible dots, but none ever came close. Their speed slowed over the next weeks, and as the concentration of galaxies increased they seemed to go by with greater speed, though they were merely closer – on a galactic scale. Regina Lane was able to determine their rate of deceleration, which was rapid, and they learned the exact moment they would fall to sub-light speed.

"Oh, My God."

Tamela Zhan was working the sensor panel. She seldom said much, and for her this was tantamount to a cheer. Sorrell and Lane sped to her side, and this time she didn't back away – much.

"We're heading right for a galaxy. We'll hit it edge on and according to the calculations Regina made we should drop out of lightspeed while still inside it."

One astronomically impossible hurdle jumped, but that paled in comparison to what Sorrell discovered a day later. He checked and double checked, uncertain whether his eyes could be trusted to see the impossible, whether his mind could be trusted to accept it. When he presented it to the others, he removed as much of the emotion as possible.

"When I studied the deceleration curve I learned where in this galaxy we would stop. The coincidence is too remarkable to be coincidence. Once I realized where we would stop, or at least slow quickly below lightspeed, the shape of the galaxy suddenly hit me. I looked at neighboring galaxies, their relative positions – we're definitely heading home. We'll be stopping in a position occupied in the Milky Way by our sun. There's no doubt."

After a moment Regina spoke. "It's amazing, but it won't matter. Relativity demands that so much time has passed, the Earth can't be there any more. We have no place to go to, at least nothing we can count on."

"I thought about that, of course. But if that were true the galaxy would have changed shape, changed position in the universe relative to the other galaxies. No, something has to be wrong with relativity because nothing has changed. I can't pinpoint an exact moment, but from the positioning I can tell, we could arrive at more or less the same time we left, at least within a few thousand years. It violates the laws of physics, but no more than what we just endured."

***

When The Terran entered the Milky Way and instead of galaxies passing across the screen it was stars, the three remaining crew members acted as though they were already home. Though they had thousands of light years to go, and

46

anything could go wrong, the scene in front of them was the most familiar they had seen in weeks. For a while they had to close the viewscreen as they passed through the central core of the galaxy, because even with the camera on the lowest possible level of sensitivity, the light from the densely clustered stars was too much to bear. The danger of some type of collision was higher, though only statistically so. Even in the center of the galaxy there was more space than spatial bodies. Their speed prevented gravity from taking too great a hold on them, and Sorrel had long since stopped worrying about such things. The sequence, the impossible series of events, brought him to the conclusion that they were meant to get home. True, members of their crew had died, or as much as died, but the ship itself, he thought, had a destiny, and he simply planned to go along for the ride.

The mystery of time-space's refusal to follow the laws of relativity still bothered him. Everything else, as impossible as they might appear, at least had an explanation. This did not. A strange and disturbing theory came to him one evening as he tracked their path through the as-yet uncharted part of the galaxy. Sitting across the table from Regina Lane, sipping coffee which once more tasted pretty good, he brought it up.

"I may have solved the relativity problem, Regina."

"Frank, as far as I am concerned, there is no problem. I don't even care about the mystery involved. A few weeks ago I accepted that I would die a horrible death. From the minute I set foot on this ship each and everything that could go wrong did, and more. But each time we fought through a problem, or watched it solve itself, I clung a little harder to life, and felt more alive. It seems obvious that we will get home, or at least close to home, and I would love to be able to try things again. I don't know if I can go to Earth, because the Brangan's could become active again, but I'm anxious to make a difference somewhere – a space station, the Moon. I'm foolish enough to even take another adventure like this. I love you, and I am glad you think you've solved the mystery, but unless it makes a difference in us getting back to somewhere familiar, I don't really care." Her smile betrayed her hard words. The expression said, *You can tell me if you want, and I'll listen, but right now I just want to feel happy.*

She had become for him the most important person in the universe, so he said nothing. *Besides*, he thought, *I'm not sure about it. I have a little test to perform.*

Tamela Zhan became more social, even sitting across the table from Sorrell on a few occasions, talking in optimistic tones. Still, she kept mostly to herself. She talked of a desert island, though she thought she might be able to handle a small town. The idea of cities and being locked in rooms filled with other people was terrifying. She's come a long way, though, Sorrell thought.

The stars continued to fly. The ship's speed dropped exponentially, but still they traveled at many times the speed of light, and Sorrell considered that their instruments were all wrong. After all, no one had ever used these computers to evaluate light impulses while traveling at such a speed. No sense thinking about it, though. They would know everything soon enough.

The last three days were the hardest. None of the three slept well, when at all, and the entire ship was a flurry of activity as every piece of equipment was checked and rechecked, cleaned and recleaned, calibrated and adjusted – all this, not so much because the ship needed such things, but to keep them busy and to pass the time.

They approached Earth's local area, and watched as the computer counted down the seconds until they would fall out of lightspeed. The sensors could not tell them details of the stellar area while still moving so quickly, so the moment they fell below the speed of light would be their first chance to see what had happened to them. The clock reached ten seconds to sublight when Sorrell hit a small switch on his panel. The incredibly small amount of power they used to operate their life support systems was ejected out the front of the ship a fraction of a millisecond before the ship dipped below the light threshold, slowing the ship the smallest bit earlier, stopping the lightspeed an incredibly small segment of time faster. No one felt it, noticed it, perceived it, but Sorrel needed it to test his theory.

The threshold passed, and suddenly the starfield was steady, stable, and still. The viewscreen ahead showed the back of a ship remarkably like the one they inhabited, floated in space for no more than half a second, then it disappeared. Immediately the communications panel erupted.

"Terran....Hannah, this is Garret. Your power levels are dead. What went wrong?"

Sorrel turned off the panel. Zhan and Lane breathed a tremendous sigh of relief, realizing they were home, where they started their journey so long ago.

"We made it," Zhan said.

"Did we go back in time, Frank? Is that the theory you were trying to talk about the other day? I saw the ship – that was us, just before Hannah did whatever he did. We went back in time a split second; that was the result of all this?"

He looked at her, and immediately knew what he had to say. "Yes, Regina. I didn't think it would be such a small amount of time, but I wondered if the result of this extraordinary trip would be a backwards step in time – and apparently it was, though I don't know how many people are going to believe the story we have to tell them. We'll have more than enough trouble explaining one dead and one mentally empty crewman, the loss of power, and more without trying to advance some wild theories about extrauniversal travel."

She smiled at him. He knew she didn't care about that right now. Her world had turned around, and she just wanted to enjoy it a little bit.

Actually, Sorrel mused, her world hadn't turned around so much as it had turned over. His test, his reason for adding the slightest boost to the ship's power in that last second, was to get the ship stopped just a little sooner. If he hadn't they never would have seen the tail of the other ship disappear, because they would have arrived at the same moment in time and the same part of space where the other ship disappeared. He had to know, and this had been the only way.

They hadn't gone back in time the slightest bit. They went forward in time an immense and unimaginable distance. As their trip seemed destined to place them back in the same place in the universe where they started, and relativity laws had to make sense, he guessed that during their time outside the universe the galaxies had continued to expand until their momentum finally stopped billions of years later, then the gravitational attraction started to pull them closer together, until one day all the matter in the universe (except The Terran) was compressed into an infinitesimal space. Then another big bang took place, and the universe started all over again, replaying itself exactly as it did before. The order of the universe demanded that they be deposited exactly where they started, their trip outside the universe governed by some law of nature or God he could never understand. Finally, plotting against the ships momentum he brought them out of the hyperlight travel a split second sooner and saw The Terran of the next universe, their counterparts, start off on the same ill-fated voyage. Did he upset things by coming in earlier? Or is that what the last Frank Sorrell had done too? What the next Frank Sorrell would do in a dozen billion years?

Those were all questions he could never answer. He decided he would never try. He never planned to tell any of this to Regina, no matter what happened. He saw a good future ahead for them. The last thing he did before stepping off The Terran is wish the crew of the next Terran luck, then he went home – or the best approximation he was likely to find.

END

THE LOOP

Over the years Jansen Hest had grown tired of listening to his friend's theories. True, Thaddeus Frisk remained the worlds most brilliant physicist and every idea he brought forth seemed new - even his most implausible theories eventually were proven correct - but for fifteen years Jansen had listened to a daily account of the most ridiculous ideas. Frisk laid out historical theories, scientific theories, all well-based in fact and researched in amazing detail, but somehow always slightly unbelievable. Jansen knew that whenever he arrived at his friend's house he would be hearing some of them again; while sometimes that made him hesitate this day he hurried, breaking into a run as often as his tired legs would allow, because Thaddeus Frisk was dying.

Jansen told himself that he should not be surprised. Frisk was old, very old; no one really knew how old he was, but his first papers had been published over fifty years earlier. Jansen, now thirty-five, had come to know Frisk while a student at the University. He took every class Frisk taught, and the two men became friends despite the disparity in their age. Now he was the old genius' best friend; maybe his only friend these last few years.

As he approached the large foreboding house, Jansen eyed the silhouette of Frisk sitting next to the window. The snow on the grounds hadn't been plowed for many days, and Jansen struggled to keep his footing to the front door. He didn't knock; he was expected. Shaking the loose snow from his coat and hanging it on the old oak hook and removing his boots, Jansen walked quickly toward the study.

"You don't have to be in such a rush, my boy," he heard the old man say. "I said I was dying, but I didn't mean this very minute!"

Frisk sat in an old recliner that looked to be at least as old as he was. His thin white hair rested on a withered face, and he used a blanket to keep out the cold.

"I didn't know you were on such a specific schedule," Jansen said. "I would have taken time to call a taxi."

Frisk smiled at the humor. Always able to laugh, especially at himself, Frisk never seemed to mind growing old, or even dying. More than accepting the inevitable, he acted as though it were another experiment. Jansen never shared his optimism about age and death, so this moment remained more uncomfortable for him than for Frisk.

"I made you a drink, Jansen. Sit down and listen to me one more time."

Jansen Hest obliged. His drink rested near the bentwood rocker he always used when visiting. It was comfortable, though not excessively so, and he enjoyed the constant motion of the chair as they talked. He sipped the drink nervously, and commented on the taste.

"I took the extra time today to brew the berries myself. This is a very important occasion."

"You mean your death?"

"No, no, my boy. I'm afraid I've deceived you, and for quite some time. You see, I don't actually plan to die. Not yet, anyway."

Jansen was confused and relieved at the same time. "Then, you are not ill?"

"Yes, yes, I am ill. Very ill. Terminally ill; in addition, they say, to being sick in the head. I guess that by this time tomorrow most people will think of me as dead. The body you see here will certainly be dead. And, God help them, people will do all the ridiculous things they do when someone dies -- preserve the body long enough so everyone can come by to say how surprised they are that I died. They say 'I just saw him yesterday!' as if I wouldn't die as long as they continued to see me once a day. They'll comment about how good I look in the coffin, when in fact I'll just look dead."

Jansen put down his drink. Now he was only confused. "I don't get it. Are you dying, or not?"

"I'm sorry, my friend. I should not confuse you so much. Let me back up a step and explain. You know already that my age has been a source of many discussions. How old am I?"

Truthfully, Frisk could be over 100, but in an effort to be cordial he knocked off a few years. "Oh, maybe eighty-five."

"You are trying to be kind. Don't, because I am not sensitive about my age and because I know I look to be much older than that. But, my son, I am only seventy-four years old."

"How can that be?" Jansen said. "Your first paper on temporal waves was published fifty years ago. Are you saying you published it when you were in your twenties?"

"I have always been a little ahead of my time, so to speak. But as well as being gifted at mathematics and physics, I've had other help. Do you recall when I spoke to you of my theory of time as a three dimensional linear phenomenon?"

"Of course. You drummed the idea into me for nearly two years. It's been years since we discussed it, but I remember many nights arguing over the entire concept."

"Then explain it to me. Let's see how well you remember it."

Jansen took another drink. *One more time for you, my dying friend.* "As you explained it, put simply, "time" as a dimension has a roughly linear shape. It has infinitesimal height and depth, and finite width. What was it, 30-40 years?"

"Yes, that right. Go on."

"You said that traveling might be possible within the width of time, though only in one direction, backward. And you stated that the slight physical presence of time allowed changes to be made in time, creating a loop in the fabric of time itself. The loop separates from the main branch of time, existing only until time moved far enough ahead to pass up the loop. If you created a loop, say, twenty years ago, that loop, separate from the main branch of history, remained in existence until time continued far enough ahead. Once another 10-20 years passed from the time the loop was created, the loop ceased to exist."

53

The old man rocked back and forth with satisfaction. "You never believed it, did you?"

"No. I never saw how you could get past the obvious paradox."

"What – the, 'If I went back in time and killed my grandfather then I could not have been born to go back and kill my grandfather therefore I was born to go back and kill him' problem?"

"Of course."

"But Jansen, if I will grant you that history cannot be changed once it has arrived, will you grant me that if time travel were possible, everything that would have been changed already has been?"

"Yes, but we have the same problem. You could not go back and kill your grandfather."

"Correct, in the basic linear model of time. But If I went back 33 years and killed my Grandfather -- or did anything at all for that matter -- I can create a loop in time. An alternative reality, if you like the term, one that exists concurrently with this one. Except that while this one -- the main reality -- cannot be altered once it passes, I can make changes in the loop, change reality, at will. I can, if I choose, kill my grandfather without creating a paradox."

Jansen finished his drink, and rose to make another for himself. "Wouldn't you then end up with an infinite number of alternate realities, branching of from one another endlessly?"

"You are forgetting the finite nature of the time line. I have discovered since our last discussions of this subject that the length of the timeline is exactly 33.52 years, give or take a few minutes. I can, from this moment on the timeline go back as far as 33.52 years into the past, and no more"

"Because beyond that time no longer exists." Jansen added.

"Correct! But, I can travel within that 33 year span, and by doing so create a loop in time. If I go back about 33 years that loop will only last a few months before time has moved ahead and erased it. If I go back 20 years I create a

54

loop which lasts 13.52 years. Theoretically I could go back three seconds and create a loop which will last nearly 33.52 years, by our measurement."

"And in each case," Jansen said, "you say that the main timeline of history remains unchanged."

"It has to, because your long-known paradoxes are valid on the main timeline."

"And you cannot go forward?"

"No. Time does not exist ahead of us."

Jansen looked down, and saw that his glass was again empty. He did not even remember drinking it. "Okay, Thaddeus. Let's say I understand your hypothesis. What does it mean? What does it have to do with you, now?"

With a wide grin Thaddeus Frisk said, "It means I have to go back and create one more loop."

"What do you mean *go back*? Are you saying that you have traveled through time before? That's impossible, because you could not return. You said yourself you cannot go forward."

"Originally I thought that the inability to go forward meant that backward travel was one way. I learned, however, that you always return to the place you started. In fact, you could travel back in time, create a loop that exists for decades, and return to where you started. From the standpoint of the people on the main timeline, the effect is instantaneous. You could travel in mid sentence, go back twenty years and live for thirteen more years in an alternate time loop, then return so quickly that you could finish the sentence without anyone seeing a difference. The only way anyone would notice a difference is if you did not return - if, say, you died in the alternate reality. In that case your main timeline body would drop dead also.

"But wouldn't the lack of return, the dropping dead, be a change of history?"

"No, it had never happened before on the main timeline. It would *be* history."

"Okay, so if I understand, you are saying that you can,

55

and have, traveled through time, always returning to the same spot, no matter how long you were gone. Always returning to the same situation, no matter what you did while you were gone."

"Correct."

"Unbelievable."

"Provable. You call me a genius. I am heralded as the foremost authority on a dozen different subjects. But do you know that my IQ scores are below average? Do you know that I learn at a slower rate than most humans? I told you earlier I had help, and that help has been *time*. I have been traveling through time for decades, accumulating the equivalent of over six centuries experience and learning. I am seventy-four years old in this body, but I have lived over 600 years in various alternative time loops."

The two men sat in silence for a long time. Jansen was torn between the certainty that his long-time friend had lost his mind, and the belief that this brilliant man might know more than anyone could imagine. "You say it is provable -- how?"

"Simply -- I will show you how to do it."

"Do you travel in time only in your mind?"

"No, although it is only your mind -- your soul -- that does the traveling."

"How do you return?"

"Simply the desire -- the will."

"You said you can die while you are in a loop. Can't you return to your mainstream body?"

"No, my boy. If you die, you die. You can only die once."

"How often can you go back?"

"Theoretically you can travel an infinite number of times, but each trip is a great strain on the mind and the mind controls the body. That strain is why my 74-year-old body looks so much older. I know that the next trip will be my last. This body will not withstand another return."

"Can you return to a loop? Can you branch off from a branch?"

"No.   The height and depth of the physical time continuum won't allow either. I have tried to travel back in time while in a loop, but it cannot be done. You can only travel from the main timeline."

"How many loops can be created? How many people can travel at once?"

"I don't know."

"Thaddeus, if this is your last trip - where will you go?"

"The finite length of physical time creates a challenge. The farther back in time you go, the shorter the span of the loop. The more recent the trip, the older I am when I get there. So, do I go back to when I was 45-years-old, live a few years as a younger man, or do I go back a few years and possibly live much longer, though as a much older man?. It presented a unique dilemma for me, Jansen, but I am satisfied that I have made the right choice. Do you recall when I told you about the night my wife Allisa died?"

"Yes, you said she was in a plane crash. That was nearly twenty-five years ago."

"I plan to go back and rearrange her travel plans, again. I've done it before, and have never regretted it. I know that since I cannot come back it will give me only about eight years with her, but that's so much more than I could have ever hoped for."

"Then you have done that before - prevented her death?"

"Many times. I was so scared that I didn't try to go back to her for years after she died. I guess I felt it was wrong, morally. The first time was twenty years ago, and we had over 27 years together that first time before the loop ran out. Each time I did it was naturally shorter and time moved forward, but each was different, and worthwhile. As I said, this time we'll have about eight years.   I didn't always go back to her. I rewrote my life a hundred times. Many people have regrets: things they wish they had done, and things they wished they hadn't. Well, I don't have those regrets because I have made the corrections. Oh, it doesn't change this timeline, but I am at peace for it."

"Will you try to come back when the loop is over?"

"I'll try. If I do not succeed, you will know when I have died."

"One more thing," Jansen said. "Why me? Why have you chosen to share this only with me?"

"The answers are obvious, Jansen. You are intelligent enough and imaginative enough to understand this. You have been a very good friend to me, in many alternate realities. And because I knew from the early days of our friendship that you have many, many regrets."

***

Armed with notes and diagrams, Jansen returned home hours later. Frisk assured him that all was well, and that they would speak again tomorrow. Still, Jansen was reluctant to leave.

He poured over the notes immediately, unable to sleep. He didn't yet believe Frisk was telling the truth, but the research both excited and frightened Jansen. Initially Frisk had developed the idea that when one traveled in time, the branch moved forward with the main timeline, until it reached the original moment of departure. Under this theory, the farther back you went in time, the more time you could spend in the alternate reality. When he tested the theory he found the reverse was true. The farther back you went, the less time you had, always limited to a total of 33.52 years. He thought he had failed in time travel for the first dozen attempts because he went back as far as was possible, and instantaneously returned. Only when he decided to try another time frame did he discover the reverse-travel nature - or rather the reverse-loop, of time travel. He had made, he said, over a hundred successful trips, during many of which he remained in until the loop expired. Other times he escaped to avoid a dangerous situation, death, or because the reality took a direction he did not want to see fulfilled.

Frisk theorized that while he maintained a conscious memory of the entire trip, the other people of the alternate realities could not because they had not transferred their consciousness there. He supposed that these events might manifest themselves as dreams, fantasies, premonitions, or echoes. But he didn't know, nor could he say whether the people would ever know about the trip, the branching of time, even after their death. He did seem convinced that this phenomenon proved that death was not the end of existence, though he had no logical way to prove it.

Jansen reached the end of the stack of papers, finding a letter from Frisk:

My Friend Jansen,

We have engaged in many fine arguments over the years, in the main timeline as well as in many others that you do not yet remember. I am confident that by now you believe me when I tell you that time travel is possible. Before I make my final trip I ask one thing of you - - come with me. I believe that if two consciousnesses' travel at the same moment they may both be placed along the same loop in time. For you, it can serve as a stepping off point, and I can be there to help you understand even more about this wonderful gift. For me, in addition to proving that two people can travel at once I would be grateful to share the loop with someone who understands what is happening as I do. It has been hard enough laying the groundwork to convince you over the years. With everyone else it has been fruitless.

I will be traveling back 25 years to spend the time with Allisa. You will be only 10, which could provide quite a few challenges for you, growing up again. I went back to being 14 once, which at the time was as far as I could reach, and I could only remain a short time. Consider it. You said that your childhood was a happy one; so reliving it again might be enjoyable.

If we are successful I will find you. I will be about 49 years old, and well known in my field.

I wish that I could have given you this information

before so we could share more trips together, if it is possible, but I could not risk letting you travel until the timeline ended after your birth. You are now older than the longest trip we could make, so it is safe. I have missed my target area more than once, and could not guarantee what would happen if you arrived at a time before you were born.

Meet me at home tomorrow at noon, and we will begin the journey.

No regrets....

Thaddeus Frisk

No regrets. Jansen stared out the window of his small apartment. His life was full of regrets, opportunities missed and chances not taken, decisions that turned out horribly wrong. Could he really go back and change things? And what if he could? If Frisk was right it would not change events on the main timeline. When he returned - if he returned - nothing would be different. But Frisk said the trips had put him at peace with himself, in spite of the temporary nature and arguable reality of the time loop.

He would be ten years old again, if he made this trip. The loop would last until he was about 18. That was well before he met Landy. He regretted letting her get away, more so than anything. Could he go back later and fix things with her? That was just a few years ago. He could create a timeline where they could spend thirty years together, as he promised her the first time. That alone would be worth any risk. If he never went back again, if he died after that trip, the greatest regret of his life would be erased.

But he could fix other things, too. His family, friends... it could all be so different.

Finally exhausted, Jansen slept and dreamed, not surprisingly, of the past.

***

Jansen arrived at Frisk's house at exactly noon. He was

afraid to be late, but just as concerned that he would arrive too early, though he couldn't understand why that bothered him. The door was ajar, and Jansen walked quietly into the house.

From the basement he heard, "I'm ready for you here, my boy." He was sure he hadn't made a sound entering the house. Jansen walked down the narrow steps, into the basement of the house. He had never been down there before, not in all the years the two men had been friends. The basement occupied the full length of the underside of the house. Jansen stopped and stared in amazement at the sight before him. The walls could barely be seen for the banks of electronic equipment that covered them. A dozen tables formed a nearly complete rectangle and each one was filled to at least eye level with computers and other electronic consoles, many which Jansen could not identify. The few windows that peeked out at the ground above had been painted black. Cords and conduits traveled across the ceiling of the basement, providing a clear path to walk anywhere in the large room. As near as he could tell there were no light bulbs in the room, but plenty of light filled the room because thousands upon thousands of small colored lights blinked endlessly from their consoles, indicating things only Frisk could understand. Up to now he had not considered the mechanics of Frisk's theories. He had been very concerned about whether it could be done, and what the ramifications were, but he had given little thought to *how* it would happen. Frisk stood inside the rectangular series of tables, staring at a small screen.

"It took quite a few years and many dollars to make this work, Jansen. You are the only person to see it, though I am not particularly concerned if someone else should; they would never understand it."

"Does it take this much technology to make a time-jump? You said yesterday that it could be accomplished with the desire, the will."

"The return to where you started requires only the desire, thankfully. It does take some machinery to make the trip back in time, though not much. I can make the jump, to

61

use your term, with a fraction of what you see."

"Then what is all this for?"

"Accuracy. The earliest trips back were rather haphazard, and I found that I wasted a lot of time - if you'll pardon the necessary pun - by missing the moment I was looking for by a week, a month, or even a year."

"But if you missed couldn't you just come back and try again?" Jansen asked.

"Every return trip causes great strain, and some damage, to your body in the main timeline. If I arrived too early for my purpose it was often much better to stay where I was, and wait, rather than endure the return. But over the years I have found ways of better pinpointing the moment I wished to return to. Forgive me Jansen, but I must continue working while we talk. I realize you have a million questions, and I'll try to answer all of them for you as we go along."

Jansen moved closer. Frisk was manipulating dials to align two lines on the computer screen. As he brought the lines together, so they appeared as one, he increased the magnification by a factor of 100 and the lines were shown to be still apart. He aligned them again, and again increased the magnification. Jansen guessed that he must be working with lines that were now less than a billionth of an inch apart.

"When these lines are aligned to within 1 trillionth of an inch we are assured of arriving when and where we like," Frisk said.

"So we can go wherever we like? In our own body?"

"Yes, in our own body, but only our body from the past. As I said yesterday it is only the consciousness which travels, and only into our own body. We can go anywhere we like, so long as we had been there once before, and only when we had been there before. Of course, once we are there we have complete freedom and can go all the places we never could before. I went to Alaska once, in an alternate reality, because I had always wanted to as a young man but never did. It was a dangerous trip, and I almost died. I fell of the edge of a cliff, and was barely able to keep my wits about me to return. It was scary. But it was worth it, because now I have done it."

Frisk made another adjustment on the screen, and the lines converged for the final time. "There, that's it! I have directed the machine to send us to a time before Allisa's death. You grew up in Ohio, and Allisa and I were traveling through Ohio not long before the flight. I'm setting the controls for that time, so you will not be far away. You'll only be 10-years-old, physically, when the branching takes place. You will find it fascinating, and frightening."

Jansen said, "I'm more concerned with what happens while we are gone. What would happen if someone came in and destroyed the equipment while we were in the past? Would it make return impossible? Would we be able to travel back again?"

Frisk lightly laughed. "You are forgetting the nature of the trip, my boy. No matter how long we are gone, we'll return to the very moment we leave, the exact second. No one would have time to affect any damage to my equipment. And the basic machinery needed to travel back is simple enough. I have left plans for you in a safe deposit box at the Western Federal Bank. And return, whenever you might choose to do so, is not dependent on the machinery. You either will it, or it can occur when time runs out on your loop."

"As long as I don't die."

"As long as you don't die. Death, Jansen, remains the ultimate victor over us. Though I think that if there is an actual personification of death, he would be displeased at our method of putting him off, and of giving life to others for a while."

"Thaddeus, this is something which bothers me. The people you meet, Allisa, your family, your friends. Are they real to you? Aren't they just ghosts of the people you know? After all, you said yourself that once you come back, and you inevitably must, nothing has changed. The dead are still dead and the different realities you lived in aren't even remembered by the living. Does it really happen at all?"

"Decide for yourself, Jansen. We're ready to go."

***

The jolt was unexpected, and Jansen Hest knew he must be falling from a cliff. He started to cry out, but stopped himself as he realized that the movement was a car, the back seat of which he occupied - or rather, which the incredibly small, frail, alien body of a ten-year-old boy occupied. He felt surrounded by the blue vinyl of the seat and the gray-blue of the fabric roof in this old vehicle. Through the window he saw the landscape pass by at a steady pace - Ohio, he knew from his conversations with Frisk. The trip had been successful! What it meant he could barely fathom, but his young heart raced with excitement, and he marveled at the opportunities which surely awaited him.

"We're almost home, Jan," he heard from the front seat. She hadn't turned around, and Jansen shook with fear, somehow believing his mother would see that he wasn't her son. But of course, she wouldn't know, as long as he acted like a ten-year-old boy. How did a little boy act? What did he say? How could he ignore the last twenty-five years of his life and experience?

"Ok, Mom," he replied, testing his tiny voice. He laughed at the sound of his own voice. This was funny! He peered carefully to the front seat, to the young faces of his parents. He forgot how young they had once looked! The last time he saw them they were much older, unhappy, and without hope for the future. It had been years, and they had long since lost contact - more regret. But here they were, in the happier days, talking and smiling. Frisk was right - they were as real as they needed to be.

Jansen knew they were returning from a visit to his grandmother's nursing home. He would liked to have come back a little earlier, but the memory of his visit was fresh in his mind, as though he had just seen her with his own eyes. Then again, he had. Frisk had explained that he wouldn't have to worry about faded memories or his youth, because everything would be there for him as though he had just experienced them

64

(because he had).   The transfer of his consciousness didn't obliterate his short-term memory, or perhaps it refreshed the old memories, since scientists had long theorized that we never really forget anything, that everything we have seen or done, barring actual brain damage, remained somewhere in our mind. Could the transference allow those memories to remain, or did it recall them from the past?   Perhaps, sometimes soon, he would study the subject.

Perhaps.

Not now.

They pulled into the large driveway to his childhood home. He jumped out of the car and stumbled to the ground, his mind unfamiliar with the light frame he now controlled. His mother giggled and caught him, lifting him to his feet. He looked up at her with amazement, and with adoration. She was a very beautiful woman. He had forgotten. He had forgotten so much.

As he ran toward the front door he picked up the latest paper, news of events and people from twenty-five years ago, freshly reported. Politics, sports, entertainment, accidents------

His eyes widened and he uttered a word a ten-year-old boy should never utter, especially in front of his parents. At the bottom of the first page sat a report of a highway accident the night before. A semi-truck had lost control and slammed head-on into a car traveling the other way. There was only one fatality, the driver of the other car....Thaddeus Frisk.

The ten-year-old boy cried. Jansen was not worried for himself; he knew, based on his being where he was, that he could return to the basement with a concentrated thought. He was convinced. He could return now, or he could spend the next eight years enjoying a youth which was the last sustained happy time in his life. He had endless options. He cried for Thaddeus Frisk, despite the man's long and satisfied life, because he had lost one last chance for a few years with his Allisa.

Abruptly he stopped crying - and understood the amazing gift he had been given. Whether he returned now, or stayed as long as possible, didn't matter. He could travel back again and change things for Thaddeus Frisk, give him more time with Allisa. Jansen had eight years in the main reality before time moved too far ahead and stopped him.

Finally Jansen Hest really understood: no regrets.

END

ARMY'S REDSTONE MISSILE AFTER LAUNCH FROM
CAPE CANAVERAL 9/17/58

THE LAST HISTORY

The blast nearly killed them both, the beam of coherent light ripping through the outer hull, but striking at an angle which spared the inner bulkhead. Rix wasn't afraid to die - no more so than anyone else, he imagined - but if he died then his passenger would die, also. That was unacceptable; if anyone could be said to be indispensable to the future it was she. Ironically, it was because she held the secret to the past.

His screen showed the positions of the remaining NG ships. Three has been defeated already, but two more still pursued him. His ship was bigger and slightly faster, so he could take no pride in staying alive so far; he had been lucky, and just smart enough. The longer they kept him in space and in their sensor range, though, the greater the chance that more NG ships would come, and eventually he would be outnumbered beyond his ability to fight. Something had to be done. He had to take risks. Grounders often thought that one could easily hide in the vastness of space, but that simply wasn't true. The problem with hiding is space is that there exists so much nothing. In nothing upon nothing, anything is easy to find, especially if you are a ship of metal and artificial materials. If one could disguise a ship to appear as rock or ice, both to the eye and to sensors, then you'd have something. Their best chance for survival would be on a planet, almost any planet. Any habitable world would work well, where air and food were plentiful. A civilized world where they might blend in with the people of a large city would be even better. Even a rock, someplace to cower in a cave, afforded better chances for survival than staying in space.

Rix jumped from his chair and staggered over the navigation panel, fighting the unstable gravity caused by so many hits and near misses. His co-pilot had been killed weeks ago, and he cursed this larger vessel that didn't have all the primary controls at one station. His passenger had tried to help, but she was a grounder, and even now was probably in her cabin fighting off the space sickness grounders often experience in their early voyages. She would get used to it, because if they lived, she would surely log many miles in space.

As he reached the panel the entire ship lurched. It was another hit, this time somewhere in the back, but the shields held. Any significant breach of the hull would turn the ship inside out, then his mission, and everything he'd worked for during his entire life, would be lost.

The sensors showed one place they might reach in time; the planet was primitive, but large. If they could get there far enough ahead of their pursuers, and put some distance between themselves and the ship, they could hold out for weeks, maybe longer. With a little luck his fellow agents - *how many were left?* - would investigate and search in the right place, before the NG did. He set the course, and returned to the main piloting station.

The enemy ships were soon out of firing range. That last hit had been their final volley, and although it might have caused damage, Rix didn't care about his ship, as long as they could land somewhere - anywhere but ocean or vast flatland; they needed some terrain.

He hadn't heard the door to the bridge open, and was startled when Alem spoke.

"The last hit - are we hurt?"

"No, at least not severely. We're going to try to reach a planet just a few light years away. We'll have to abandon ship and try to lose them on the surface for as long as we can. If help is coming at all, it won't be for a while. Go down below and fill two packs with as much food and water as you can. I'll look for the best landing spot. Strap yourself in - we can't afford to be injured because we need to get far away from the ship, quickly. I'll be down as soon as we've landed."

Alem nodded, but said nothing more. She had gotten used to being ordered about, though she didn't like it. She once more observed this strange man who weeks ago had stolen her from her home and family with his claims of protection. He

68

had refused to tell her why, but she quickly learned that there someone was out to kill her, and they would have succeeded had he and his partner not been there to stop them. The other man was dead, and she had cried over that many days, but there was no point in it now. She wanted only to survive, and to learn what this was all about. Rix seemed to have the answers, but he wasn't telling.

They were out of immediate danger, and Rix watched the woman walk away. Smart, brave, and although not well educated, Alem had more common sense than did some experienced agents he knew. She was attractive, too - not a mere youth, but still in her prime of womanhood, yet never married and never with child. These few facts he learned during some of the quieter moments, but not much more. He kept from her the most important things he knew about her.

The planet was called Tombstone - An ominous designation, and no explanation for the strange name appeared in the files. Rix wondered if it meant some unknown danger, but they couldn't afford to remain exposed any longer. He brought the ship down in a dense forest within hours of rivers, hills, and, further along, mountains. He hadn't decided where they would go, and the NG surely wouldn't know. The landing was rough, though his concern was only for his passenger, not the ship. The ship would be destroyed the minute it was discovered by the NG. Then, the hunt was on.

Rix and Alem stepped out into an alien forest, a dense world of deep blue trees partially blocking a pink sky. The packs were heavy and uncomfortable, but he hoped not enough to slow then down. "How long do we have?" Alem asked.

"If there were no ships approaching we that didn't detect, we have three or four hours, maybe a little more. In that time we have to put some distance between us and the ship, and remove every refined metal we have. In fact, the sooner we do that the better. Their scanners will detect any processed metals and give them a clue as to our direction. Not having metal will make our survival tougher, but make their search difficult as well." They inventoried their possessions, and walked away from the ship with their clothing, backpacks of synthetic fibers carrying their food and water, and one small pistolaser which Rix wanted to keep just for a while, until they could survey the land. They marched Northeast, toward the mountains.

They reached the base of the first mountain as the sun of the planet began to set, turning the sky a deep red before heading toward black. Rix noticed a light on the horizon that he assumed to be his ship; the self-destruct program, which he set to engage when anyone entered, reducing everything to radioactive slag. *Let them search that for clues*, he thought. With the ship now gone the NG would begin looking for smaller metal signatures, so the gun had become a liability. He opened the casing of his weapon, and carefully made some connections inside, then tossed the pistol to the ground between them. The gun emitted a growing hum, and Alem backed away, but Rix took her arm lightly.

"Don't worry – I set it to overload, but there's no danger."

Alem had never seen such a weapon before, and it had scared her from the beginning. She had imagined it's destruction would come with fire and explosion and a great release of energy, but as she watched the metal glowed a pale green light, the surface seemed to melt, and the gun began to fall onto itself, becoming smaller and less distinct with each passing second. Almost before she knew it the gun was gone, only a very small patch of slightly burned earth marked where it had been.

"The small amount of heat it emits when it implodes could have started a fire, so I had to watch until it was gone. No trace of the processed metal remains; the elements have returned to simpler forms. We should be untraceable by their sensors. They will be after us in force, though, so we had better cover some ground and find decent shelter until help arrives." He started to say *if it is coming* but thought better of it – after all, if it is coming, it is coming. If not, they would learn that soon enough.

The two hiked far, with no timepiece or method to measure the passing hours, and no idea the length of night on this world. Once they encountered a creature something like a small lion, and Rix cursed himself for too quickly disposing of his blaster; but the animal didn't recognize humans, and was equally afraid, eventually moving off in search of familiar prey. Finally they happened upon a small cave almost completely covered by the trees, ideal for their purpose. Almost without a word they entered and set up their meager camp for the night – or as long as they needed to use it. Alem commented on their good fortune in finding the shelter, about which Rix nearly laughed out loud. They had been running for weeks, shot at, their colleague murdered, their ship destroyed, their chances of survival slim, and yet she found some reason to feel lucky.

They sat now, their backs resting against the cold stone of their cave, unfamiliar sounds of nature echoing through the tunnel from outside. Desperate to find a distraction from their situation, Alem asked Rix to tell her about himself – most importantly, why he was here, on this world, with her in tow. He thought for a minute, decided this was as good a time as any, and began.

He started with the day the Historical Preservation Society (HPS) was formed: As the human race reached out, beyond the boundaries of its solar system, history became harder and harder to teach. The people of Earth had little interest in their planet's past, with so much happening in outer space. Colonists refused to see the significance of Earth's history, believing that history started with the day their particular colony was founded. The HPS was formed for the purpose of researching, studying, and most importantly preserving history for future generations. The first compilation was published in book form and the computer disc in vogue at the time, covering not only the best of Earth's historical writers, but the works of scholars from all of the major settlements. As the colonization expanded, as populations increased, the size and scope of the HPS grew with it.

Then they met the alien races, and history was changed; first came the story of the contact, later of the wars and then finally peace, and the HPS had to preserve not only the story of the human race, but also the newly encountered races. This was the Golden Age of the HPS, when the value of their work and the resources available to them grew. Rix spent almost an hour telling Alem stories of the old masters, their research and their adventures. She listened quietly, smiling at his enthusiasm for what most considered a dreary life.

The Golden Age lasted for nearly two centuries, but politics soon outpaced technology, governments fractured over the interstellar distances and the dark ages of the galaxy began. The HPS tried to protect what had become the story of hundreds of small kingdoms, republics, dictatorships, social experiments, and economic fiefdoms; but the work had moved underground, with chemical modules shared between members of a semi-secret, tolerated but never supported, organization. The HPS nearly collapsed a hundred times, the membership falling quickly due to political unrest and apathy. No complete compilation existed, but some massive module collections survived these terrible years.

The greatest threat in those days was the forgeries, and Rix spoke of these with great hatred in his eyes. The value of a previously unknown module could be worth millions, and with the inability to verify so much information in enemy systems, thousands of false histories were distributed. That was when the HPS members started to change from scholars to agents of truth.

Slowly the political climate changed and over the next few centuries the galaxy stabilized, communication improved, and the HPS saw a resurgence of their power. Membership was restricted, the requirements for the various departments strictly controlled. Rix's great-grandfather was an agent, and his great-great uncle one of the most respected researchers of his day. It was thought that one day in the galaxy a complete history could again be compiled, accurately researched and completely verified. Work began on that galactic history, slated for publication as a micro-chem-module, to be the greatest achievement of the HPS.

Then the New Government took over. How it happened was still being studied, and the complexities could fill more volumes than any previous story known, but when the NG came to power over most of the systems the first thing they did was rewrite the story of the whole galaxy. They claimed the right to rule, by genetic superiority, historical precedence, and legal tradition – legitimizing NG rule to future generations. The only problem was: all of that was a lie. Even if the NG was good --- something few outside the government itself would suggest --- their claim to destiny and right was untrue, and the HPS became their greatest enemy.

Faced with hundreds of years of effort and sacrifice destroyed, the HPS went completely underground. The NG published their false histories, designed to serve their needs, and the HPS covertly tried to keep the facts – including the story of the NG lies and atrocities – in front of as many people as possible. Their tactics changed by necessity – no longer could they just research and verify, now they had to break laws, beg, borrow and steal capital, even from time to time become violent, in the hopes of preventing the true history of the galaxy from disappearing. The HPS no longer just preserved history – they created it.

The first recorded assassination of HPS members by NG agents was over 75 years before. Since that day the war had raged, with terrible casualties on both sides. The NG resources were much greater, but the HPS found allies among the common people. Even those who cared little for history cared even less for the NG. Over time, though, the HPS was weakened; often entire libraries were destroyed and complete HPS cadres killed. It became a desperate race to find a method of preserving history, one which could not be eliminated, even if every HPS agent were killed.

Just over twenty years before, the first DNA-encoded subject was born. The female offspring of HPS volunteers, the child was altered *in vitro* to contain, encoded directly into her genetic make-up, the basic history of the entire galaxy. Hiding the information in a person, was a tactic that would take the NG years to discover, and it was believed by then that the small group of carriers would have bred in sufficient numbers that finding all of them would be impossible. In a few centuries, a population that had the history of the galaxy forever inside them, would be impossible to subdue, spread over thousands of systems. It was an incredible plan, with great chance of success.

But someone told. No one was certain what happened, whether an HPS agent was tortured for the information, or even bribed (which Rix thought impossible) – or perhaps an NG agent had somehow infiltrated an HPS cadre. However it happened, the NG suddenly knew the names and locations of the nearly 2,000 carriers ranging in age from 23 years on down to infancy. They started killing carriers efficiently and without explanation to the population. The encoding facilities were destroyed, the records eliminated, and within a few years the entire galaxy seemed doomed to historical genocide.

"At last count," Rix said, "only 14 remained alive, and with them rests the fate of the galaxy. We've managed to remove then from the population, but getting them to safety has proven to be more than a little difficult."

Alem listened, interested in the fascinating tale, but also concerned with every small noise coming from outside their sanctuary. Incredible, she thought, that a small but determined band of teachers and scholars would encounter such a force, and almost emerge victorious. They were bound to fail, however, the NG being too powerful, too all-reaching to be kept long at bay. It sounded as if their quest was nearly over.

"Fascinating. How do the - what did you call them, carriers? - feel about being manipulated before birth. I mean, the parents were able to choose, to volunteer, but obviously the infant had no idea what was happening."

"True, but does any infant really have a choice in the life he - or she - is destined to live? I didn't know I would be born into a family of resistance to the NG. The poverty-

74

stricken child doesn't choose it, any more than the wealthy landowner's child knows what might be in store for him. It is all an unintended gamble, and what choice do we have but to work with the cards we are dealt?"

"A very strong argument, but nonetheless I would hate to be ---"

Her expression changed. For the moment she had forgotten their plight and his refusal to explain why he had taken her away from her home world so abruptly. The stories he told struck her as curious, but unimportant, yet now she realized that -- no, that could not be.

"These carriers, when are they told what they carry?"

His eyes darkened. "Not until they have to be."

Silence hung over the cavern.

"No," she said. "I'm not one of those. I'm just a normal person. You've made a mistake."

She rose and paced back and forth in front of Rix, refusing to look at him.

"It's no mistake, Alem. Not only have you been closely watched for your entire life, I personally tested you once you got on my ship. Please, try to understand what an honor it is to -"

"HONOR?! You call this an honor, to be hunted down like a Procon Dog for something you don't even understand, or care about?" She pointed at him. "You made a mistake. I am not some 'carrier' for you to save and protect. I'm not one of those."

"You are."

"I'm NOT!" she cried. It was unlike her to be so emotional, even in a dangerous situation like this. Her anger, she knew, came from knowing he was right – that this incredible story, based on what she had experienced in the last few days, had to be true. She tried to recall if anything in her life, anything she saw or heard, could have warned her about this. Had she noticed anything peculiar, which now could be explained by her being watched, studied? She couldn't find anything in her memories that would have given her a clue. As

Alem stared at Rix, tears rolling down her cheeks and her expression stone, she believed him, hated him for what he had told her, and realized she wouldn't see her world again - if she survived.

Rix looked at her; she had crossed over, past denial, and he now faced his most difficult challenge with her – making her want to live, showing her the value of what she was, helping her to appreciate it. Their chances of rescue were slim; their chances of being discovered by the NG strong. He had tried to protect her by himself, and failed. Perhaps together they could do the job. Rix felt the weight of history on his shoulders, and saw that Alem now carried the weight as well.

He wanted to reassure her, tell her that everything would be just fine, but then he heard the sounds of the search party, the orders and cries of the NG commander, just outside the cave. His mission had failed; his charge was doomed.

***

The trip had passed like so many others – long, boring, and fruitless. Gare liked solitude most of the time, but he was beginning to tire of wasting his time. Sure, the money was good – great, in fact – and he was hailed as a hero for his efforts whenever he returned home, but the feeling of uselessness invaded his thoughts, entered his dreams, ruined his days.

His small scout ship settled into orbit around the planet, the thirtieth such world on his latest tour. He set the sensors to their highest setting, to compensate for the lush forests that covered so much of this planet. A beautiful world, he thought, but like so many others full of life this world would read dead to his instruments, which looked only for a certain kind of life, a certain signature that no one had found in centuries. Gare double-checked everything, then settled into his bed for a long nap.

The alarm didn't register in his sleeping mind right

away – it was unfamiliar. He knew every sound the ship could make, and at some point in his travels had occasion to hear each one, but not this. He jumped from the bed, staggered across the floor of his small ship and reached the navigation panel before he recalled that he **had** heard the sound before - in spacedock, when testing the systems. There was the signal! It was weak, it certainly wasn't genuine, but here, on this planet devoid of humanoid life, out in the middle of nowhere, was a faint signal of the type he had been looking. If accurate it would be the most important discovery in history. Centuries of searching, centuries of the slimmest hope ---

No, he couldn't allow hope to invade his work. There had been signals in the past on other ships, reports of signatures that turned out to be false, either mechanical failure with the sensors or some reading that couldn't be ruled out because of the limits of technology. Once, a few decades ago, a searcher discovered bones that read positive. If the DNA could be extracted from those bones, the entire galaxy would rejoice, but once closer examination was made the readings proved false.

It had simply been too long. The NG, the long-dead and long-despised arm of a failed Empire, had won after all. Gare, like the others in a dwindling group of Searchers, existed merely to prove that to the galaxy.

Gare had trouble locking down the location of the reading, which further convinced him that this was futile. Still, he was duty bound to immediately report, and he would investigate while the recovery team was on the way. He would be able to update his report and turn them around soon enough. He sent his sensor readings, his coordinates, and completed a short message:

"--- similar to those the sensors are designs to detect. I will go planetside and determine what is causing the diffuse signature so it can be added to the exclusion list for future missions.

While I have the channel open, I may as well report that this will be my last tour. I'm retiring. It's time for me to look toward the future, not toward a past we'll never find again."

Gare began the long checklist that would result in resting his ship on the surface. He located a clearing not far from one of the areas where he found the greatest concentration of faint readings. Even if remains were dispersed through animal activity, it could never account for such a wide pattern – and besides, animal activity and bacteriological activity would long since have degraded the DNA. This whole thing was just a waste of time.

He landed. The planet contained lush vegetation, rich atmosphere, and a wealth of insect and animal life – a wonderful place for people, though none had ever settled. He stepped out of the ship and began his trek through the grass and trees, looking for the signal he knew he wouldn't find.

But he did find it. His portable sensors showed the signature coming from the very rock beneath his feet. It wasn't strong, probably from something imbedded far below ground, but it was very definitely the right signal.

Then it moved.

He lost the signal, but found it again a few minutes later – or was it another signal altogether? This one moved, too, and Gare tracked it for ten minutes before it changed direction and eluded him. Gare leaned against a tree, shut off his sensor, and pondered. Did the water contain some chemical, some liquid flowing underground that mimicked the signal he sought? The dense rock beneath the soil of this rich planet interfered somehow with his understanding.

Suddenly he was running. He didn't know which direction to run, but he was in full flight, looking for something. He ran for miles in one direction, then changed to a new direction without reason. He had no clue where to go, but knew he had to find one. Twice he fell as his feet became tangled in branches, and he gained a large knot on his forehead, which he barely noticed. He did notice, however, the cave opening not thirty yards away, and he rushed headlong toward it. He switched on his lantern, prepared to face any creature whose home he had invaded. Gare entered the cave and followed the largest passageway.

He stopped suddenly, the answers to all the questions he could have asked, and many thousands more, stretched out before him. He stood on the edge of an underground cliff, overlooking the most magnificent city he had ever seen or could have imagined. Spires of glittering minerals reached up from the floor of the massive cavern, stopping just short of the ceiling above; granite roads criss-crossed the city in geometric patterns of great symmetry; thousands of people walked those roads, entered the buildings, interacted with one another across miles and miles of this underground metropolis.

Gare didn't need his instruments; he didn't need to verify anything. He stood hundreds of feet above the floor of the cavern, but his eyesight was good. The population was diverse, but here and there he saw the unmistakable resemblance to Rix in men who passed by. He couldn't help but be reminded of the image of Alem in the faces of young women he saw. They weren't dead ringers, but there was no doubt from whom these people descended.

History was saved.

He had so many questions, but for hours just watched the city below, staying out of sight until the time was right to make contact. Gare speculated on what must have happened so many hundreds of years ago. Rix and Alem eluded their pursuers – that was plain. Or perhaps they didn't completely elude the NG, because there was enough diversity in the characteristics of the city dwellers to account for more than one pair of ancestors. Maybe there was a battle, with Rix and Alem the victor. Or they lost, but somehow managed to survive. Maybe there was a truce, some meeting of the minds, some deal reached. Gare couldn't say for sure, but what was obvious was that Rix and Alem did survive, and over the years they started a new race on this planet. They stayed underground – probably at first merely to escape the NG and protect their lives. Is it possible they still fear assassins?

No matter the reasons, below him there were hundreds of thousands carrying the critical gene structure of Alem – a whole world teeming with living, breathing chronicles of the history of the galaxy, long thought lost.

Gare had a few more minutes before he must venture back outside to wait for the recovery team. He spent that time contemplating his announced retirement, with great joy.

END

FIRST FREE WORLD SATELLITE - JUPITER C #2 TEST 54 (SY)
JANUARY, 1958

CONEY ISLAND CIRCA 4001

"Over there! I want to go over there!"

The seven-year-old's grip tightened and pulled the man along. His father's feigned resistance only made the effort more enjoyable. Hol Granthem looked up and the square building of metal with the grinning clown and the bleeding goat perched on top.

"Why do you want to go there to eat, Danal? There are so many places to choose from."

The boy never slowed down. "Teacher said that in the olden times people ate animals in places like that. I want to see what it is like -- can we, Dad?"

Already tired from their long day at the amusement park, Hol knew that arguing about dinner would just consume more energy. Besides, he'd always wondered what the ancient primitives really ate. This could be fun.

"Okay, we'll go," he said, "but after that we have to go home. Your mother will be waiting for us, and we have to get to bed early before our flight back to Mars in the morning."

The structure bore the most comical rectangular shape; an inefficient design, but then again, it was supposed to simulate the Ancient ways. Metal and stone walls - *who'd ever heard of such a thing?* - gleamed white under the light of the dome. The sculptures that surrounded the building didn't offer an appealing sight, but if you wanted authenticity, you had to sacrifice some common decency, especially when dealing with the Ancients.

They entered the building, and were greeted by a young woman in the same grinning clown costume. "Welcome to the Slaughterhouse!" she said with a huge smile. "Is your son over five years old?"

"I'm seven!" he said proudly, stretching his small frame to look even taller.

She bent down and placed something into his hands. "That's good. We don't allow the really young kids in here, because some of the practices of the Ancients were a little rough."

Hol was concerned. "We're not going to see any of the rituals, will we? I mean, roadkills or touchdowns, or anything like that? We just wondered what the food was like."

"Don't worry," she said. "We wouldn't resort to such things. No one really wants to see stuff like that. But the food items are interesting, and even if they don't taste exactly like the Ancients ate, we're proud of the presentation."

She explained the restaurant and showed them to a table with a plastic cover of red and white squares. Of course, modern restaurants would never have something so bold, but Hol remembered reading that the red was used to mask the blood marks on the table. How strange that the Ancients would make such a celebration of killing and ingesting animals, then try to cover the spots. Then again, much of what the Ancients did was confusing.

Hol turned to his son. "What did she give you, Danal?"

The boy opened his hand, and in it were four gleaming metal disks of various sizes. Each had the portrait of an Ancient king on one side, and on the reverse was the mutilated corpse of an animal lying under a pair of arches. These, the hostess had explained, were called money, and were part of the custom known as tipping, or getting screwed. The more you liked the meal, the more of these disks you left for the servers. In the days of the Ancients, at the end of the night the server with the most disks was rewarded, and ate the remains of the server with the fewest disks. It was barbaric, but Hol imagined it ensured good service at all times! Their server, who pretended to be very focused on the disks, winked at Hol and gave them each a thin sheet of paper that showed all of the items available. Hol was most interested in something that simulated the goat on the roof -- beef, it was called. So, he ordered a "beefurger." Danal chose a long gray meat nestled inside a piece of bread, called a "hot dog." Hol smiled, and wondered if young Danal realized that "hot dog" is what the Ancient pets were called also. It was customary to follow your ordering by saying "with fries and a coke"-- a blessing of some kind, he imagined. After a while their food came, and they began to eat.

The pictures along the wall fascinated the youngster. Hol explained that the Ancients had ancestors and deities who they called on in times of great crises or anger; they were called the Oh My Lords. It was hard to explain Ancient religion to such a young boy, but Danal was very smart, and wanted to learn. As Hol enjoyed his beefurger (which tasted very much like his typical wheat casserole) he did his best to teach.

"Danal, as you know, the Ancient Latins were considered the best scientists; the Ancient Africans were the best artists; and the Ancient Anglicans the adventurers. Each Ancient race specialized in some specific skill or science; because of that they surpassed us in many ways, although they were, of course, exceedingly cruel. The Americans, for example, were amazing politicians, but were also cannibals, known for inviting refugees from all over the world only to throw them into a huge melting pot. The Ancients believed that they knew everything there was to know; but sometimes, when they faced real trouble or wanted to conquer one another, they would call on their Gods. That one" -- he indicated a rather fearsome looking creature attacking a village in a colorful but violent painting -- "Was known as God Damn. His Latin name was Damnation, of course. He was the God of anger and rage."

"How about this one, Dad?" The boy indicated the painting directly above their table. A tall bearded man (truly an Ancient, to still have hair!) looked lovingly on a crowd of unhappy people, who had their hands outstretched as if waiting for something.

"Oh, him. You'll learn a lot about that one in school. He's the God of Questions and Uncertainty. He was called Geez; his ancient Latin name was Geezes. Whenever the Ancients felt they were treated unfairly, they would call to him to find out why. They would say 'Geez, why does this have to happen to me?' or 'Geezes, can't I ever get a break?'"

"Did he answer them, Dad?" A sharp young boy, Hol thought, to ask such questions.

"Well, of course the Ancients believed that he did, though we know in our enlightened day that it was just myth."

"Why did they believe he answered them, or how would they know?"

"The Ancients were very easy people to please. If they got what they wanted - for example if their enemies died or if they received a lot of these disks - they were said to have a prayer, which meant a good day. And they thanked a God. If it didn't happen, they never blamed Geez or the other Gods, because they believed that they must not have worked hard enough since 'the Gods help those who help themselves'. In those cases they accepted that they didn't have a prayer, and they still thanked God."

"The Ancients were funny people, Dad."

"Yes, they sure were, Son. It's good to know that 2000 years from now people won't be able to look back on our time and make fun of it. Now hurry up and eat your dinner."

"Hey, Dad! How about if we don't leave any disks for the server tonight? Maybe he'll say 'Geezes, why does this have to happen to me?'"

Hol smiled. His son showed great curiosity and intuition. Surely one day Danal would become a scholar, and although the truth about the Ancients had long ago been revealed, he would enjoy passing that story on to future generations.

END

HE SANG FOR HER

No one talks about it – well, not much. Sometimes, when it gets late and only a few people remain in the bar, a few select people, people who were there, the subject comes up. Even then the conversation is strained, short sentences, never saying much.

"Do you still remember?"

"I can't forget."

"Why do you come back? Sometimes I'm afraid to."

"I'm afraid not to. Seems disrespectful."

"Me, too, strange as that is."

Seldom is more said than that, a few vague comments that no outsider would understand.

To anyone visiting for the first time, Jaclyn's Place Bar & Grille is a typical place, much like any other Midwestern small town bar; an island bar with stools lined up alongside it, a small kitchen for fired foods and grilled burgers, a jukebox in one corner and half dozen tables. Neon signs advertise the popular brews, and a small television set plays the live sports or the latest news. Three nights a week – Monday through Wednesday - the customers gather for karaoke, though not nearly as many as used to.

It was that typical-ness that drew Andy to Jaclyn's Place one night. New to town, slow to meet people and unsure of himself, Andy looked for somewhere he could both be a part of the crowd and blend into it. He wanted to be involved, but not so much that he couldn't disappear into the woodwork if he felt uncomfortable. He first stepped in on Thursday, and returned every night, so by the time karaoke rolled around Andy felt comfortable, though still a little like an outsider.

Andy sat in the corner, in the shadows, and watched. The parade of singers, wannabe singers, and no-chance-of-ever-being-singers that first night fascinated him. A woman offered the worst version of Bad, Bad Leroy Brown Andy thought he could ever hear; one young man, almost totally deaf, nonetheless sang the latest pop song with great enthusiasm; old women imagined they were Patsy Cline, young men envisioned themselves the next Elvis, and a the occasional individual managed a passable version of their favorite song. The host called for applause after each selection, reminded the customers to tip the barmaids, made the occasional quip, sang a bit herself, and introduced the next singer. To Andy it was a new world. Most of the customers sang, and in recognizing their own weaknesses they understood those of others. It was the effort that was applauded more so than the result. When the night was over it seemed everyone went home satisfied - even Andy, who just sat there and watched.

He came back every night, seeing some of the same people and a few new ones, but just sitting and watching. The host, Donna, talked to him, made him smile, but never tried to coax him to sing as she did the others. Andy had been alone for quite a while, and it was easy for him to develop a liking for her, but he considered her to be "out of his league" – though he couldn't really say himself what that even meant. A little confidence, he thought, would sure be a nice thing. For weeks he sat and watched, pleased but not really happy, contented but never satisfied.

One night a few weeks later, after one or two beers more than usual, and on a night where fewer people than normal visited the bar, Donna glanced over at the corner, gave him a nod and a "why not" expression, and Andy picked up the songbook. Not familiar with much new music, he picked something from his youth, something he knew because he'd heard it hundreds of times over the years – if not on the radio, then in his memories. In what seemed like only seconds he had filled out the little slip, turned it in to Donna, heard his named called, and was standing there at the microphone, belting out a tune previously done only in the shower or in an empty room. Almost as quickly, it was over. Donna smiled – she had a terrific smile – and then Andy was back in his corner, applauding for others.

That night at home Andy decided it wasn't too bad, considering he'd hardly sung a note in months, maybe years. He'd try it again sometime soon. It was worth it, to see Donna smile.

Andy started singing regularly, sometimes pretty well, sometimes not so well. He learned the songs he could do well, and those he'd best stay away from. He knew mostly the older stuff, but that was okay – Donna always liked what he picked and often said it was her favorite. He began thinking ahead to the next day or the next week, choosing songs and practicing them over and over before the next karaoke night. He didn't kid himself that he was a great singer. When it came off well he was happy, but when it didn't, he took it in stride. He came to know the people, and they came to know him, but while he enjoyed it when they came up to him and told him how well he'd done, how much they enjoyed it, that wasn't what mattered. He sang in part for himself, to express through his favorite songs those emotions he had kept buried and those he never knew he had; but mostly he sang for Donna. She didn't know it, of course – to tell her that would destroy the purity of what he imagined he felt. He'd come to know her a little bit, and while he knew it was silly to think of the few hours they spent together each week, mostly from a distance, as being important to her, he hoped that what he sang a few times each night, a few days a week, might stay with her throughout whatever the main part of her life actually was. As before, Andy was pleased, though not really happy - somewhat contented, though not satisfied.

His barfriends (as he called them, because never once had he seen any of them in town) knew of his growing fondness for Donna. A few encouraged him, though they knew her even less than he did, merely voicing their desire that he take a chance, maybe wanting Andy to have that happiness that few of them had themselves. That they knew made Andy uncomfortable. That Donna probably knew was almost certain, although she never let on, their host-singer-barfriend relationship never changing.

For months he had been singing for Donna, singing to Donna, and wasn't really sure she knew it. Who she was, and what she might want from life, he had no idea. What she thought of him he didn't know – perhaps she thought of him as he thought of her, though it was just as likely that she thought of him as one more singer on karaoke night who needed a little encouragement to get up there. For weeks on end that uncertainty kept him from considering changing things, yet suddenly this one day, that things should remain the same seemed wrong. He could end the day rejected and feeling more alone than ever, but he knew that by the end of the night something would be different, and that was enough for the moment.

It was during his second song that he asked her out. She smiled, and just said, "sure." Of course, with all the noise in the bar, there was never time for more than a few words anyway, but Andy only needed to hear one. Later that evening they added a few more words, and dinner for the following Sunday was set.

The next few days were nervous, but something truly wonderful happened when he picked her up. The moment they started talking all anxiety left. He immediately knew that he could be himself, and didn't need to try to impress her. She was equally relaxed, and there were no awkward moments of silence. There were moments of silence, to be sure, but just smiles and enjoying the moment.

"I was glad that you finally came up to sing," she said. "I knew you would, eventually, but I didn't want to have to drag you up there."

"I'm not much of an entertainer," Andy replied. "At least, not vocally. I'm a writer, and I guess I've always been more comfortable when I can organize my thoughts and edit them, look them over, express them just the way I mean to. Singing….well, that's always been a little too uncertain, a little too….wild."

"But you took to it so naturally. I mean, I wouldn't sign you necessarily to a recording contract, but you do the songs well, like they just come to you."

Andy laughed. "Naturally? What you don't see is that I spend hours during the week looking for the right songs, practicing them, picking which I can do with the least chance of trouble. I labor over every word, over every note. I toss half the songs out after trying them half a dozen times, and I spend the afternoon watching the clock."

"Wow – um.....I don't even spend that much time getting ready, and they pay me for it." She laughed, too, then smiled and took his hand. "You don't have to go to all that trouble, you know – just to sing for me."

The night went well, and although neither of them said so, Andy knew that there would be more nights like it to come. As he dropped her off at home he said, "See you tomorrow. I promise not to practice too much."

She looked confused for a second. "Oh, I almost forgot -- I won't be there tomorrow night. My mother's birthday, a family thing. Someone will be filling in for me. You'll still sing, though, right? Please?"

Disappointed, but not willing to disappoint, Andy said, "Sure – a song or two."

They kissed softly, and said goodnight.

Andy floated through the next day and walked into the bar wishing he could talk to everyone, tell everyone what they would probably never know – what a terrific person had been standing in front of them night after night. Everyone knew that he was there in large part to see Donna, so when he sat there smiling, listening to song after song with a wide grin on his face, even though she wasn't even there, people wondered. A couple hours passed before he realized he'd forgotten to put a song in – and he had promised her to sing.

He sang confidently, in good voice. He enjoyed it – nothing was going to dampen his spirits that night.

About half way through the song during an instrumental break, Andy did something he never did: he looked away from the lyrics on the screen, and looked up at the clock. It said 10:38. He turned back to the screen, had trouble focusing, felt a wave of confusion, and started the song again.

Only no words came out.

Andy thought he just hadn't heard his own voice, but he saw people starting at him, some amused, some confused. He tried again. He formed the words, his breath was there, but nothing came out. Andy stopped singing, coughed, cleared his throat, and said, "Sorry – lost my voice for a second."

He sounded fine, so he started singing again. But again, nothing came out.

Andy spoke into the microphone ---- "You can hear me talk, right?" Enough people nodded, so Andy knew he had his voice. He tried the song again – nothing. Finally he gave up, shook his head, and walked back to his chair in the corner.

That was strange, he thought.

He sat there for a while. He'd say a few words, and then try to sing a couple notes. The words came out fine, the notes, not at all. He thought about whether he should see a doctor, but how could he even explain it? Who would believe it? What would Donna think?

Andy felt uneasy. Not surprising, he thought, consider the strangeness of what had happened – but no, it was something more.

He heard a scream.

One of the barmaids dropped the telephone she'd been using and collapsed. Andy joined the group that tried to help her, get her to a chair, and get her a drink. He heard what everyone else did.

"About an hour ago there was an accident. Donna's car flipped over – she's dead!"

Through a cloud, Andy stood. Everything was fuzzy. He heard the words, but what he heard couldn't have been real. Voices crossed one another in slow motion, and images blurred in front of him. People stared at him – *why were they staring at him?* – and looked at the clock, then back at him. The clock on the wall clicked loudly, and Andy's eyes were drawn to it.

11:38

There was a funeral – Andy didn't go. The bar had a special memorial, but he didn't attend. He never went back to the bar, and a few weeks later he left town. No one ever saw him again.

"I heard he went to some town in Kentucky – works in a factory, making frozen pizzas or something like that."

"I heard him talk before he left town. He was at the Post Office, getting his mailed stopped."

"So what? We all know he can talk. Just can't sing."

"I know. He sang for her."

END

LAUNCH OF SNARK MISSILE 12/16/59

WHAT WOULD YOU DO?

IF YOUR WORLD WAS A HUGE SPACESHIP, 230 YEARS OLD AND FALLING APART, WOULD YOU RISK THE LIVES OF MILLIONS IN ORDER TO SAVE IT?

***

IF YOU WERE THE LEADER OF A FEW HUMAN-INHABITED PLANETS, SURROUNDED BY HOSTILE ALIEN SPECIES, WHAT SACRIFICES WOULD YOU MAKE TO PROTECT THOSE WORLDS? WHO WOULD BE EXPENDABLE?

***

WOULD YOU BETRAY THE MOST IMPORTANT PERSON FROM YOUR PAST TO RESCUE THE MOST IMPORTANT PERSON IN YOUR FUTURE?

These are just some of the questions answered in the novel SECRET ENEMIES. While it is the story of epic battles and sweeping galactic conflict, it is also the story of a few people. How these people make the decisions they must make is the focus of this fascinating book. In the meantime, galactic armies battle, planets explode, adventures are tackled, and loves are lost and found again -- enough action on every page to keep SECRET ENEMIES in your hands from beginning to end.

SECRET ENEMIES

BATTLE FOR THE GALACTIC ARM

AVAILABLE AT
AMAZON.COM

OR FREE SHIPPING
DIRECT FROM
THE AUTHOR
$14.99 - DELIVERED

RICHARD BUCHKO
109 FIFTH STREET #1
CALUMET MI 49913
734-934-7036
richardbuchko@gmail.com

CHAPTER TWO
THE PLANET IDONA
YR:MO:DY
12:14:03

Among certain Concourse worlds, rumors about the huge ship Teretania were more common than facts. Even in the most modern areas of the planet Idona, Teretania was mostly legend. So when the ship made her first visit to this world, it was an historic day.

In some areas, though, it was a day like any other day simply because it had to be. Renck Alletson and his young son Caleb worked hours on end weeding their crops. In a good year they would make enough to feed the family well through the long Idona winter, and perhaps sell the surplus in one of the larger cities. Most years, like this one, they hoped to grow enough to survive. The hot blue sunlight beat tirelessly on their shoulders as they removed, one by one, the unwanted growths that threatened to steal precious water from their seedlings.

Caleb, now seven and in his second full year in the fields, shielded his eyes from the sun to see the massive Teretania, miles above the surface of the planet, yet bigger in the sky than the sun itself. The ship was no thing of beauty. Even to the backwoods-educated Caleb, it seemed a jumbled mass of metal without design or forethought.

"Father," the boy began, "what would it be like to live on a spaceship?"

Renck had never ventured far from the farm where he was born, so he could not answer the question truthfully. Like many, he had heard the stories and rumors about Teretania. He heard that people were not allowed to grow old, that a person was killed if he failed the rigorous annual tests each citizen must endure. He also heard that until that day no luxury was denied to the people of Teretania. Men had as many wives as they could afford, and the women, said to be the most seductive in the galaxy, lived for no purpose other than to provide pleasure for the men. Violent games were conducted daily, with death to the loser, and all the property of the vanquished going to the victor. He had heard that Teretanians traveled from planet to planet, trading for or stealing what they wanted, then leaving their waste behind as they sped off to another world. He heard of this and more, and believed it to be true, but Caleb was only a boy and didn't need to hear of such things.

"I hear they don't work very hard, Caleb - certainly not like we do, and for that they are to be pitied. They are lazy and give nothing useful to the galaxy. Son, it is on your own planet that you will always be able to find a purpose in your life." Renck believed what he had just told his son, so leaving out the details was for his son's own good.

The image of Teretania, clouded by atmosphere and the distortion of Idonian heat, was unusual; it appeared to Renck as a giant conglomeration of twisted metal and disorganized patterns. As he puzzled over this a great flash of light burst from one corner of the ship, powerful enough that for a split second it outshone the sun, then it was gone. Renck returned to his work.

"What was that flash, Father?"

Without looking up again, Renck replied, "It may be a signal, or perhaps they are celebrating their arrival. I don't know Caleb, but it is nothing we need to worry about."

"It must be miles long and wide!" said Caleb.

Renck became angry. "Well, whatever it is, it's certainly not a matter of life and death! Removing these weeds is, so let's get back to it. There's supposed to be rain next week and I want all the weeds gone by then."

***

TERETANIA

Inside Teretania, near the explosion that had been viewed by the farmer and his son, hundreds of people lay wounded in a large room; some lay dazed while others were seriously hurt, even dead. Through the glow of the corridor behind them, smoke rolled into the room just over their heads and molten metal splashed into the room. The medical staff, too few and unprepared for the flood of injured, struggled to save those they could. Firemen carrying suppression equipment streamed past the injured without looking. The corridor ahead seemed to be a wall of orange and blue fire.

The ship shook, and amid screams the firemen retreated from the blaze. They ran past the injured again, and as one fireman passed by, a young man grabbed his leg.

"Where are you going? There must still be hundreds of people still inside!"

The fireman glanced back at the blaze, not looking at the man while he said, "This is a large Hydrantium fire. It's gotten too big. A Hydrantium blaze of this size can use up a year's supply of oxygen in a few hours. We have to seal the section off and let the fire burn itself out in space."

Another group of emergency technicians rushed into the room and placed huge metal plates against the entrance to the corridor; powerful arc welders began to fuse the plates to the walls, blocking the entrance. In seconds the job was complete, the smoke and heat of the inferno suddenly gone.

94

The wounded man stared in horror. As the fireman tried to leave, the injured man, ignoring his own dire condition, reached up and grabbed the fireman's arm.

"You can't do that! There are people I work with in there – people I know!"

The fireman looked at him for the first time, saw his serious wounds and grimaced, saying, "We have to protect the rest of the ship. Once the fire has died out we'll go in and see what can be done. It's necessary, for the good of everyone."

The man released his hold and sank down in both exhaustion and despair. He struggled to take a deep breath and said, "Can't you do anything?"

The fireman looked over at the metal plate, the cold gray surface that separated them from the disaster. "I'm sorry," he said slowly. "You should count yourself lucky to be on this side of the wall."

***

Garl Zavis read and re-read the official report of the explosion. Over 300 people had died and hundreds more were injured. One of the newer engines - this one less than 20 years old - had ruptured under the field variances of hyperlight travel. The report from Teretania's Tech Union cited this as a one-in-a-million occurrence; Zavis recalled that two similar explosions killed people just last year. He went over the Tech Union report, then reviewed his own report, prepared by Arch Durdik and his group - two reports about the same incident, and two entirely different sets of facts. Where Arch's report may have been pessimistic it was only slightly so. The Tech Union report, thought it didn't misstate any hard facts, seemed not to recognize that this was not a singular event; it was a pattern.

Zavis put both reports away and stared for a moment at the walls.

He sat at the head of a large rectangular table. Four chairs lined each side of the table, but Zavis was only expecting a few Technos. The table and the room were not particularly opulent. The table was made of oak, from Earth. The chairs were covered with a common but durable hide from the Lapis Bears of Izar. Blue walls displayed the crests of each of the 17 independent nations that had battled and negotiated for control of Teretania during the wars of a decade ago. The unique feature about Zavis' meeting room was that it remained large. At one time on Teretania everything was big; space was available to everyone, and for any conceivable purpose. Now, though the population of the ship grew only slightly each year, space was harder and harder to preserve. As areas of the ship become unusable, dangerous, or sealed off to prevent contamination from some disaster, Teretanians were forced closer and closer together, in less comfortable and increasingly dangerous situations. Someday soon,

Zavis believed, this room would have to be reduced.

The door opened and eight figures in blue Techno uniforms walked quickly into the room. Eight, Zavis thought, is a good sign. The Technos always increase their numbers when they are worried, and their decision to fill the table meant, he hoped, that they were taking this seriously enough. Leading the group was Carol Tho, Chief of the Teretania Technical Union, but the others were all new to him. Tho was a tall, middle-aged woman, handsome, with long red hair, but always without the smile necessary to make her really attractive. They entered silently and sat down. Tho spoke.

"Mr. President, we received your request for a report on the incident at Reactor Engine 14, and your request for a meeting. What questions can we answer for you?"

Zavis stood, a reflex to mask his anger at her statement. "Ms. Tho. First of all, this was no request and I won't hide behind the pretense that it was. I have the right to this information, as well as to call you here. I also had the 'incident' - as you call it - investigated by my staff, and I have their reports for you. Copies will be arriving shortly. But let's start by redefining what we are talking about. This was no incident - this was a disaster."

"Of course, Mr. President, I was using a technical term -"

Zavis interrupted loudly, "300 people died! If we are going to reach some reasonable conclusions about what happened and what we are going to do about it, we all have to recognize that! To hide behind terms and semantics, or to try to downplay the severity of this 'incident' is an insult to each person who lost his life that day, and an insult to the families who will never see them again."

The room remained silent for a moment, but a Techno finally said, "Field variances are a fact of hyperlight travel, Mr. President. We do all we can to prevent the weakening of reactor integrity, but despite our precautions they will give out on rare occasion. Nothing can prevent that."

"What's your name?"

"Willom Derr, Radiation Monitor Second Class."

"Between you and me, Mr. Derr, how often in one million interplanetary trips should what is described as," Zavis read from the Techno report," 'a one-in-a-million occurrence', happen?"

Derr read the report, but did not look up.

"Mr. Derr, how many reactor engine explosions have you personally monitored over the past year?"

"Three."

Another Techno broke in. "We sweep all Reactor Engines with sensor probes during every planetary orbit. We have never allowed one to operate if a weakness is found. We repair it and test it thoroughly before it is put back on line. We do our job, Mr. Zavis."

The door to the meeting room opened again and Mar Coss entered with a small stack of papers, which he handed to Zavis. Zavis indicated for

Coss to take his seat at the other end of the table, then made his reply.

"You sweep all reactor engines during every orbit. I'm sure you also sweep the solid fuel engines, our single Einstein field reactor, and of course you monitor hull integrity at all times. Yes, you do your jobs. But in the last two years we have gone from fifteen reactor engines to twelve, because three have blown up. We've lost almost 5% of our usable ship volume due to various hull problems, and over 500 people have died as a direct result of these explosions. Yes, you do your jobs, and that is the problem."

Carol Tho said, "You confuse me. Are you complimenting us, or accusing us?"

"The problem, Ms. Tho, is that you are doing your job, but it is the *wrong job*! You repair, you replace, you improve systems when you can, but you - and all of us for that matter - are failing to protect Teretania in the process! You have put your interests ahead of the ship's."

At that the room erupted. Technos screamed at Zavis from every side. Tho finally regained the floor, and stood to face Zavis.

"Why would you make such a claim? For over a half-century we have protected the lives of Teretanians, including our own families. How can you accuse us of such cold motives?"

"Because your organization," Zavis said calmly, "with all of its responsibilities and resources, has failed to realize that when reactor engines are swept, yet they continue to buckle under field variance, something else is wrong. Engine number 14's output was increased during our voyage to Idona, am I right?"

Derr replied first, "Yes, but only by 3%."

"That was 3% more energy than that particular engine had ever put out in space, and higher than it ever been tested. Why?"

"I made that decision," Tho answered. "We needed the extra output to reach Idona on schedule. It was a minor increase, incapable of causing a problem."

Zavis's face turned red. "The damn thing exploded! Last year Number 6 blew up, after being safety-swept while in orbit. The output, not coincidentally, had been increased beyond previous limits on the trip before it exploded. Number 11 blew up, shortly after a large increase in output. It, too, had been sensor swept. The bottom line is, we are going too fast. Hulls are buckling, people are dying."

"We are not insensitive to the deaths, Mr. Zavis," said a previously silent Techno. "We are touched by them as well, and are taking steps to increase our monitoring of critical areas of the ship."

"The problem is that *all* areas of the ship are critical, and the sensor sweeps you do will not prevent this from happening again. This is an old ship, the oldest known to be in operation in the galaxy. Factor in its great size, ancient composition, and the stresses it must endure, I think we are incapable of judging with any reliability what systems are safe." Zavis reached for the papers on the table and began to send them around the table. "If you will all take one copy of the report and pass the rest..."

After a moment Zavis continued. "As of today the office of the President controls both the scheduling of Teretania stops and all engine outputs."

Among the screams that followed Tho was heard loudest, perhaps because when she stood the others drew back. "You can't do that! You don't have the authority!"

"By our Constitution the Teretania Technical Union is not a governing body," Zavis replied confidently. "And all scheduling and power decisions rest with the Executive branch. Only a vote of the Senate can override those decisions. As President of Teretania I have the authority, gentlemen. You have not had to accept it during prior administrations, but you work for me. The Tech Union, of course, continues to handle all maintenance and repair functions; but I intend to use my authority to protect this ship."

The room fell silent again, then Tho spoke softly. "Gentlemen, please leave Mr. Zavis and me to discuss some matters. I will be in touch with you later."

As the Technos filed out, Mar Coss stepped over to Zavis. "Should I leave, Garl?" Coss was currently Vice President of Teretania, a quiet man, committed to Zavis and his policies. Both men were in their early forties, with strikingly similar features common to Teretanians of the same clan.

"No, Mar. She can tell the others to go, that's up to her, but you know I want you in on all official discussions, and I guarantee this will be official."

"Then you're recording?"

"I'm recording."

Tho walked over to the two men.

"Mr. Zavis, what I have to say is off the record, but I think you should listen closely."

"Ms. Tho, no conversation is off the record."

"Have it your way. Your desire to rebuild Teretania is well known. Your criticism of the Tech Union is public knowledge. As temporary acting President your authority is tenuous at best, and the Senate is going to view this as nothing more than an attempt to discredit us and to secure as much power for yourself as possible before the upcoming elections. They will not support you, neither will the people. You have a fanciful vision, Mr. Zavis, but the real future of Teretania lies in preserving and improving what we have, both the history and the technology. Movements like yours are keeping that from happening. You can't win."

"If you believe that, Ms. Tho, then make a complaint to the Senate during their session next week. The election takes place in a few months. You have those two opportunities to make your point. In the meantime, I control the ship, and any Techno who doesn't comply will be replaced, even if I have to go down to Idona and pluck farmers out of the fields to run the ship."

Tho turned to leave. "Those two opportunities are a long way off. Be wary of other opportunities that might present themselves."

As she disappeared through the door, Mar Coss stated matter-of-factly, "That was a threat."

Zavis grinned. "Yes, but carefully worded. She understood my comment about nothing being off the record."

"She knew you were recording? Why did you tip her off?"

"Because right now I hold the cards. You and I know what has to happen. We can't do without the Tech Unions if Teretania is to be rebuilt. They have knowledge and experience we don't. They'll need significant help with new technologies from the Concourse, but the Tech Union is critical to our plans. If we can get them to realize that we aren't trying to eliminate them, that they don't need to be suspicious of our tactics or our motives, perhaps they'll stop trying to hold the ship together with glue and prayers."

Mar interjected. "You're thinking that if we can't win you want to have better relations with the Tech Union?"

"No Mar, if we don't win, Teretania is dead. Teretania can be a part of today's world of Gravidrive and forium, but she can never be repaired, not safely. We can't cover up the weaknesses of old technology. She has to be rebuilt before it is too late. I just want someone at the Tech Union to know we're willing to work with them."

"Do you think Tho got that message?"

Zavis didn't answer. Arch Durdik, Zavis' political strategist and on-staff engineer, rushed in with a report for Zavis. He was short, and at least ten years older than the other two.

"Garl, this is what the Technos planned for the stop at Izar. There's no question that with Number 14 gone we can't hope to keep this schedule. We risk another explosion, maybe not on this trip, but the fluctuations we'll encounter by increasing the loads on the other engines might push us past the point our hulls can take. We would be lucky to make it a year without another devastating accident."

Zavis heard Arch, but continued to study the report. "I'm going to see Tho. Maybe without others around she won't feel the need to posture; maybe she'll see some sense."

"Forget it, Garl," Arch said. "We'll be at Idona for three more days. You've already exercised your authority. Did you record it?"

"Of course. I'll make you a copy tonight."

"Good. Let them stew in it for a while, and you can tell them what to do with their own plans later. Right now you have to write that speech. You're on Vid in less than six hours."

Frustrated, Garl Zavis left. Mar Coss watched his friend go. He was unsettled, distrusting Durdik more every day. Coss knew that Arch Durdik had received the report on the Techno plans for the Izar trip hours earlier, but had waited until after the meeting to give it to Zavis. As Zavis left, Coss turned to ask Durdik why he held back the information, but was shocked into silence. Where Arch Durdik had stood seconds before now stood a shimmering light that gradually took a vaguely familiar form.

The figure spoke. "Holding human form is difficult. I didn't think it could hurt to reveal myself to you."

"Who are you - Where is Arch Durdik?"

With a grotesque smile the being answered. "Arch doesn't exist - never did." He stood slightly taller than a human, with the blue-green color, long snout and tail of a Brodian, but the lumpy formless torso and legs of a Gorup. "I'm here to oversee the takeover of Teretania."

Breaking free of his shock and suddenly realizing the danger he was in, Coss ran for the door. A bolt of energy slammed into his body from the direction of the creature behind him, holding him in place. Unable to move and in great agony, Coss was barely able to hear the alien speaking.

"I am a new being, a rare combination of a Brodian male and a Gorup. It's a difficult mating, since the Gorups are asexual beings, but a mixture which gives me some advantages." Mar Coss felt a burning throughout his body. "Through a combination of shape-shifting and subtle hypnosis my Hybrid associates and I can pass as humans for limited periods of time. You see, your political party's cause of rebuilding this vessel will succeed. In my disguise as Arch Durdik and with the help of other Hybrids I will see to that."

Coss's body flamed. The plans of the Brodian-Gorup Hybrid were the last words he heard.

"Teretania will become a great vessel. When it is complete, and we take it from you, it will become the home base of our invasion force!"

Coss disappeared in a final agonized flash, and the human form of Durdik reappeared. "Too bad you won't be around to see it, but you were getting suspicious and your death suits my plans too well."

END CHAPTER TWO

Made in the USA